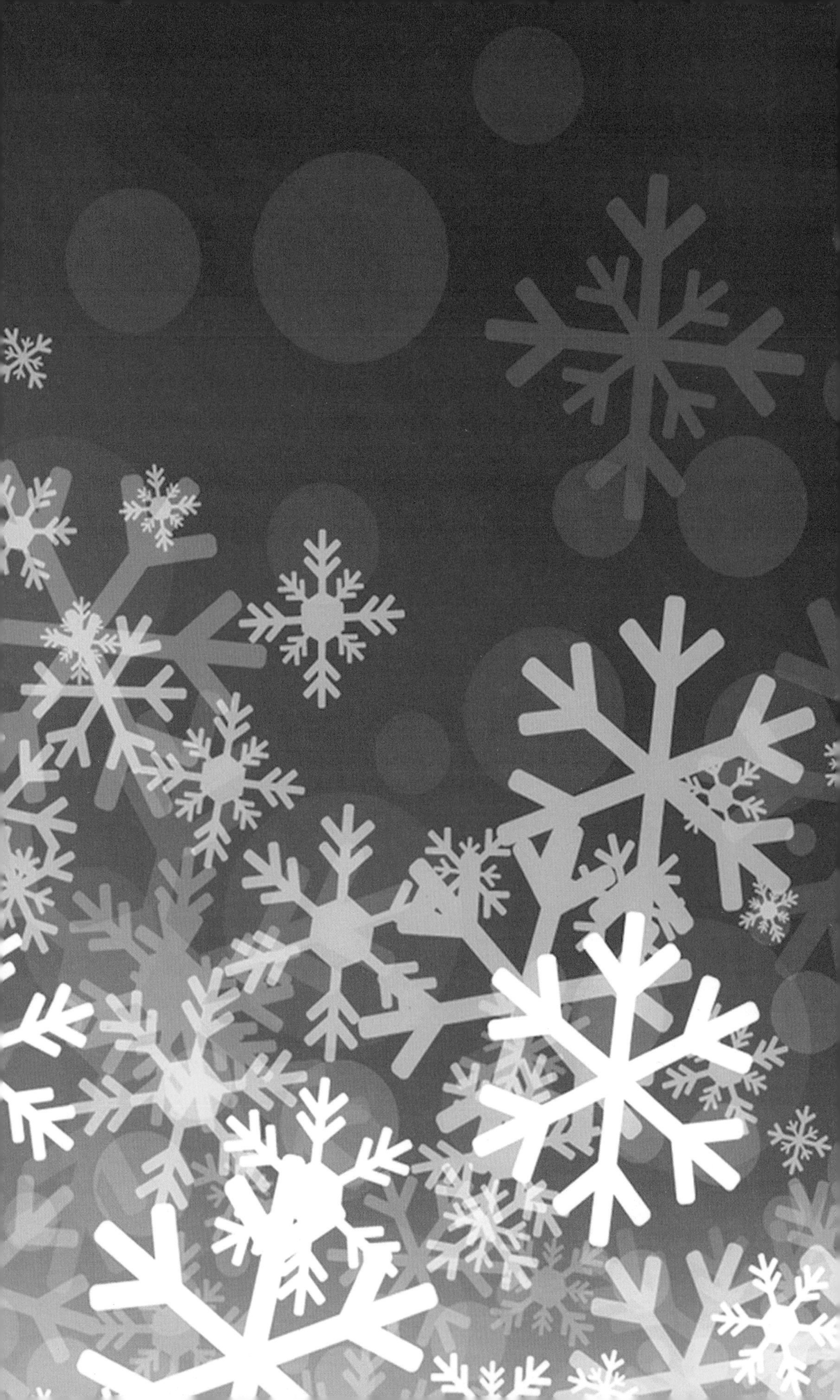

ZAG HEROEZ

MIRACULOUS™

SANTA CLAWS

BASED ON THE ANIMATED SERIES BY
ZAG ENTERTAINMENT

CREATED BY
THOMAS ASTRUC

STORY BY
THOMAS ASTRUC, FRED LENOIR & SÉBASTIEN THIBAUDEAU

COMIC ADAPTATION BY
NICOLE D'ANDRIA

ART ARRANGED BY
CHERYL BLACK

SONGS COMPOSED BY
NOAM KANIEL & FRED LENOIR

LYRICS BY
FRED LENOIR

LETTERED BY
JUSTIN BIRCH

ACTION LAB

Publisher/ CEO - Bryan Seaton
Editor In Chief - Shawn Gabborin
Danger Zone - Jason Martin: Publisher
Marketing Director/Editor - Nicole D'Andria
Executive Administrator - Danielle Davison
Akumatized! - Chad Cicconi
President of Creator Relations - Shawn Pryor

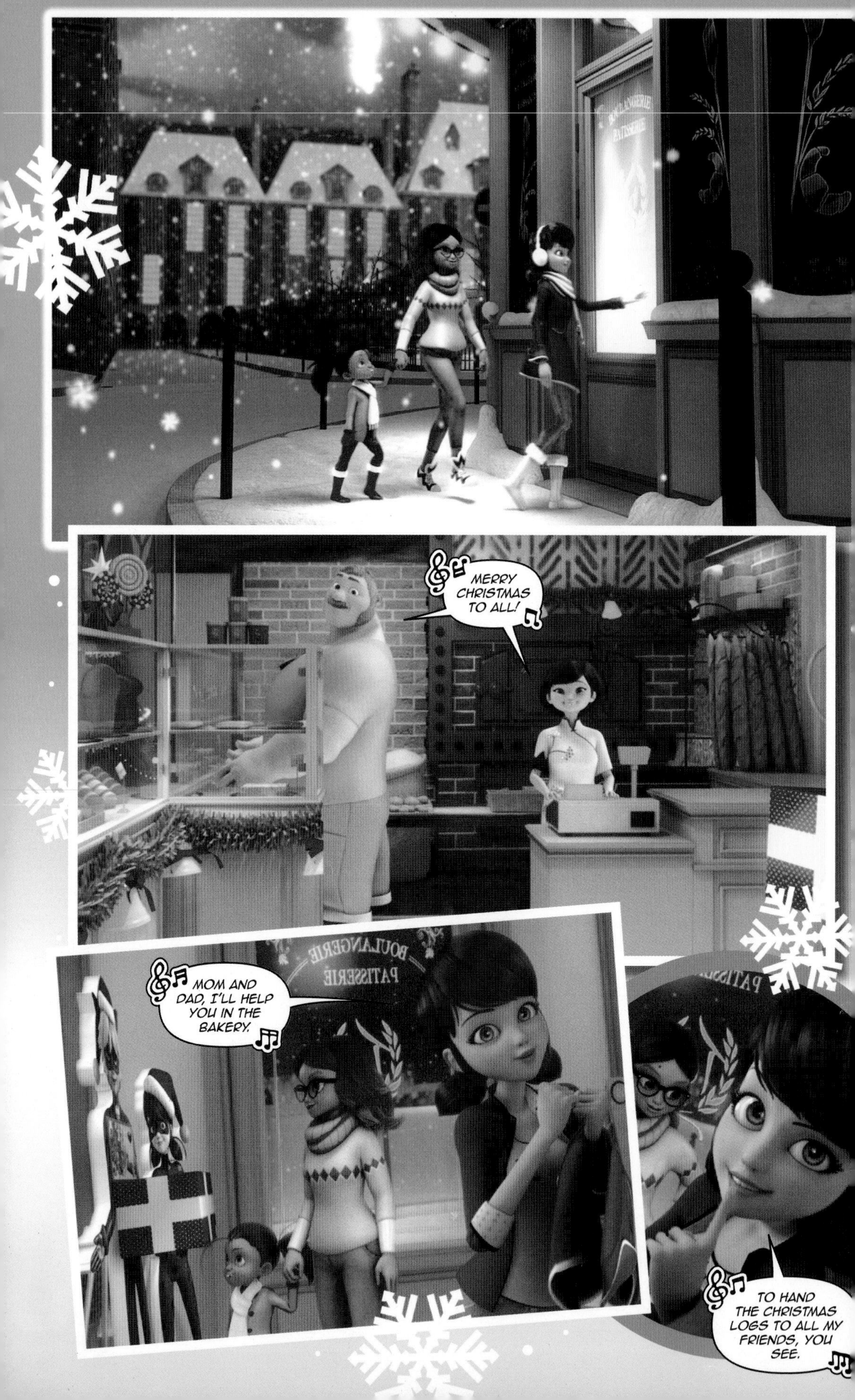
BOULANGERIE
PATISSERIE
MERRY CHRISTMAS TO ALL!
MOM AND DAD, I'LL HELP YOU IN THE BAKERY.
TO HAND THE CHRISTMAS LOGS TO ALL MY FRIENDS, YOU SEE.

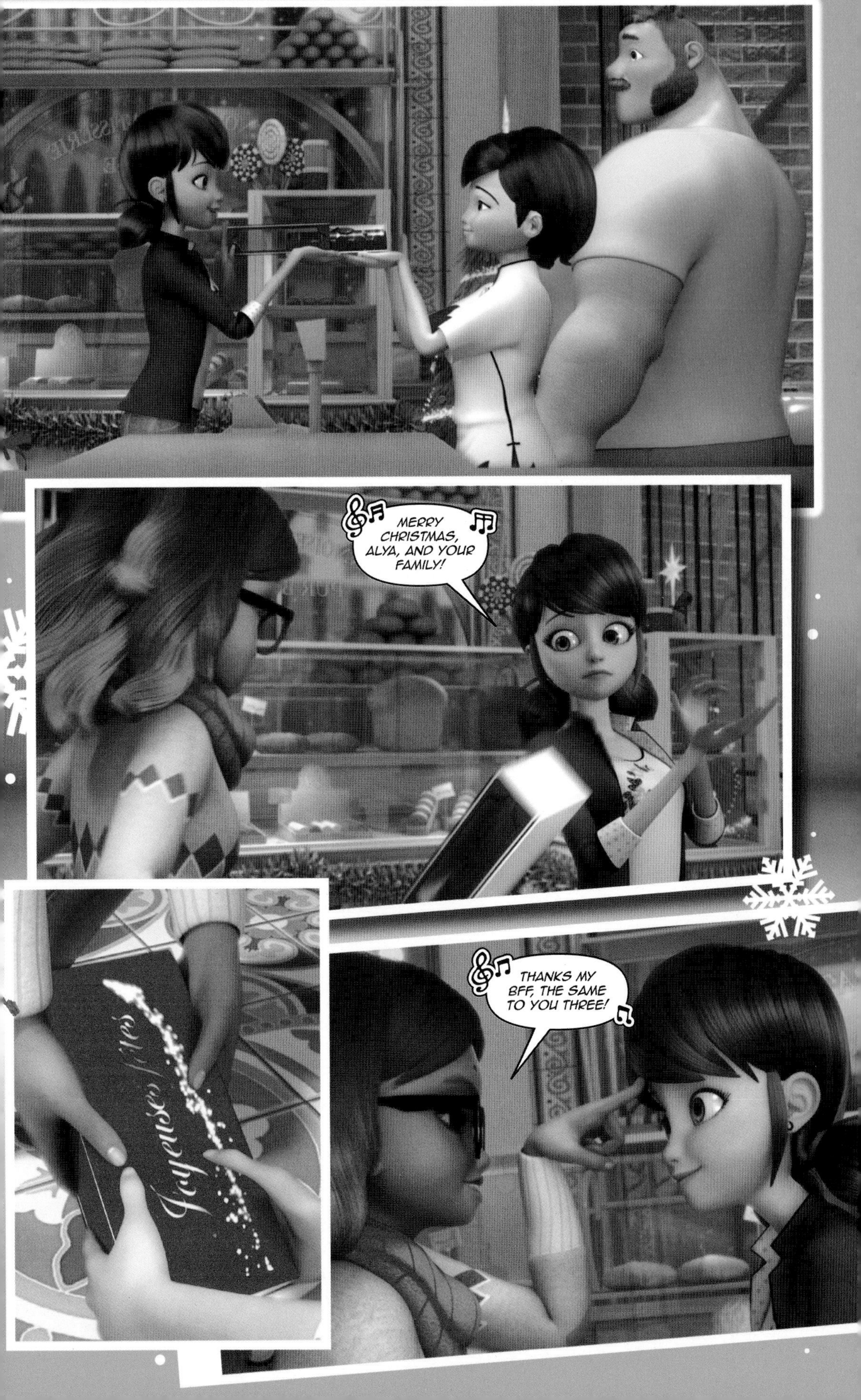
MERRY CHRISTMAS, ALYA, AND YOUR FAMILY!
Joyeuses fêtes
THANKS MY BFF, THE SAME TO YOU THREE!

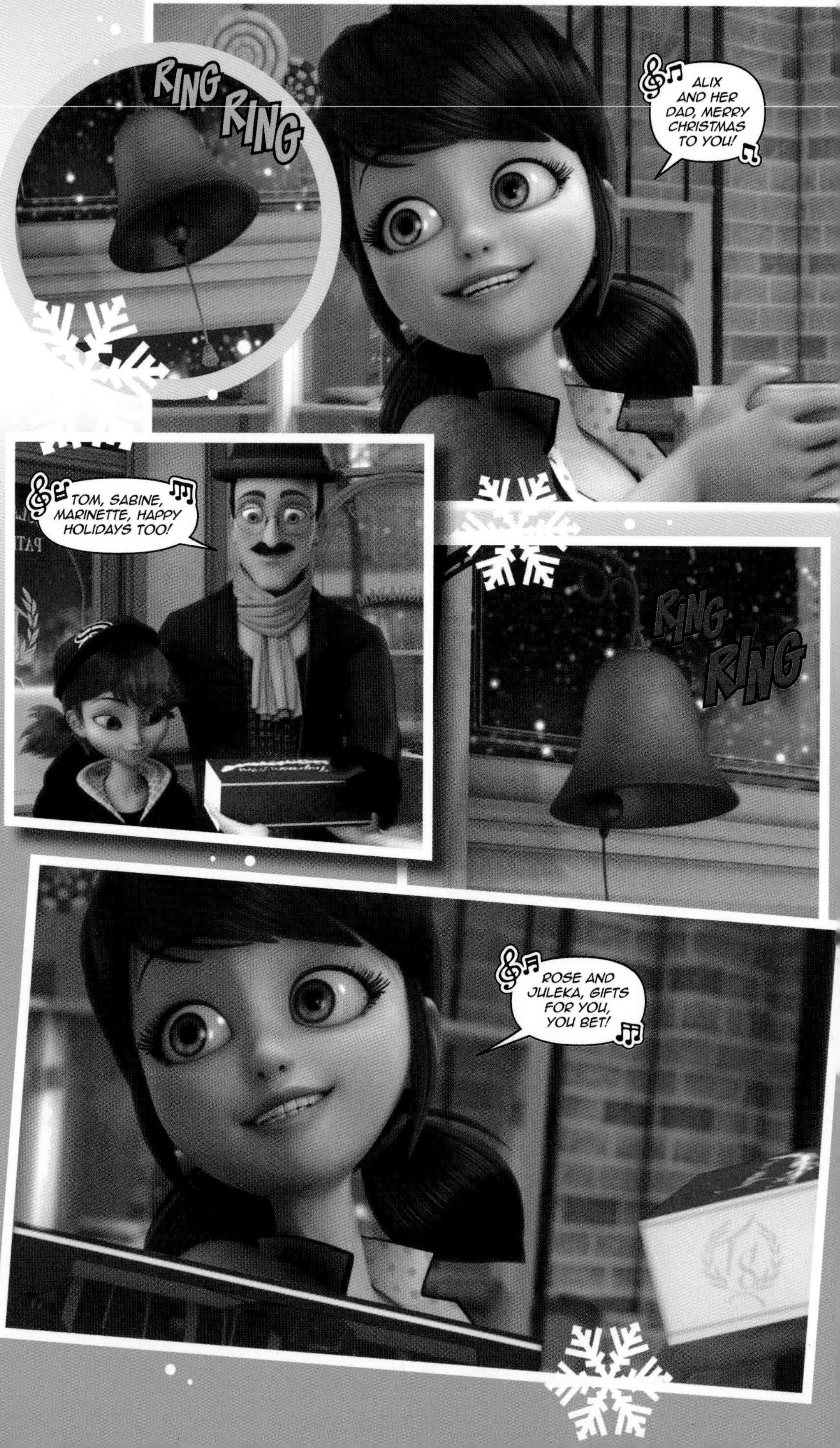
RING RING
ALIX AND HER DAD, MERRY CHRISTMAS TO YOU!
TOM, SABINE, MARINETTE, HAPPY HOLIDAYS TOO!
RING RING
ROSE AND JULEKA, GIFTS FOR YOU, YOU BET!

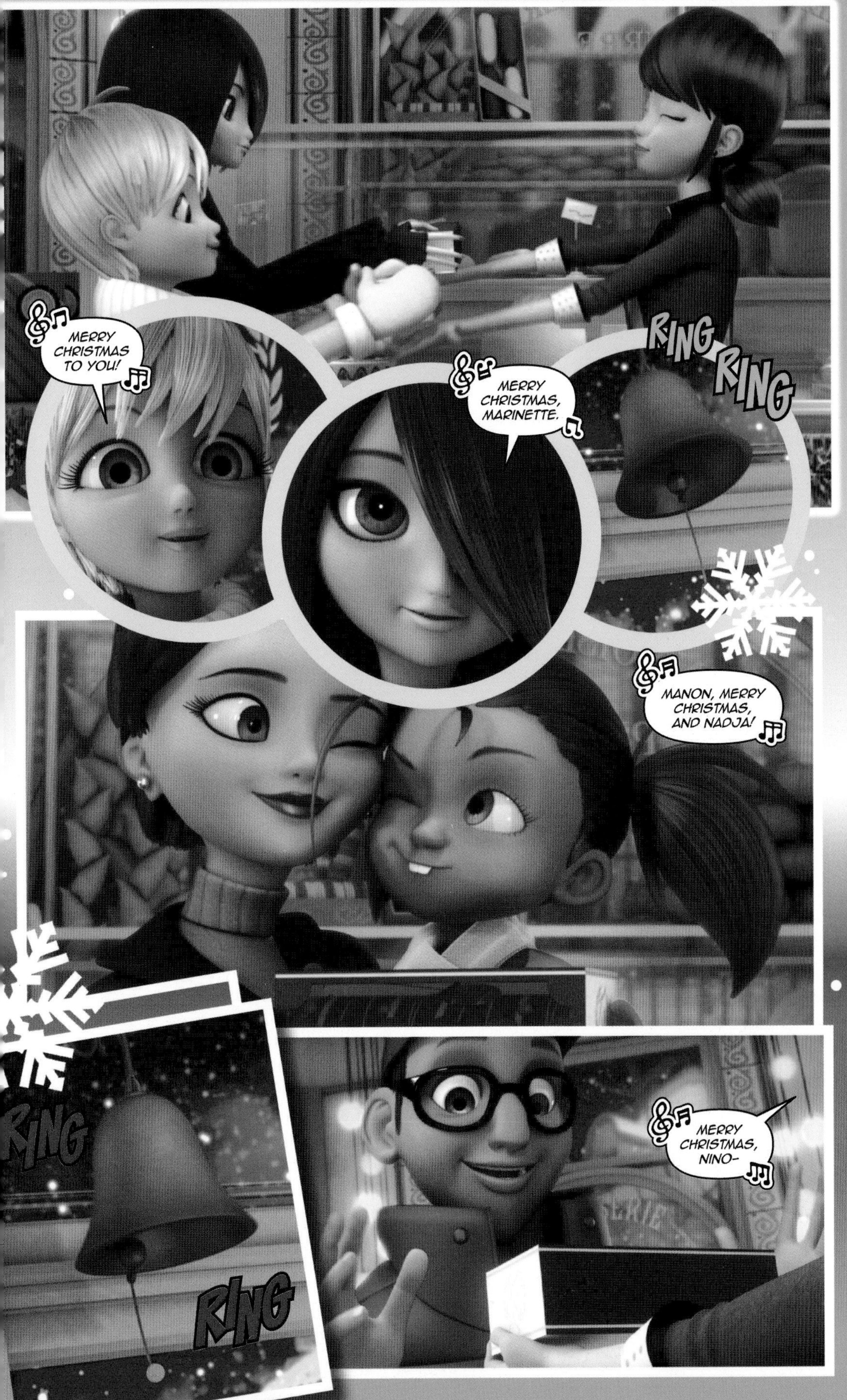
MERRY CHRISTMAS TO YOU!
MERRY CHRISTMAS, MARINETTE.
RING RING
MANON, MERRY CHRISTMAS, AND NADJA!
RING
RING
MERRY CHRISTMAS, NINO-

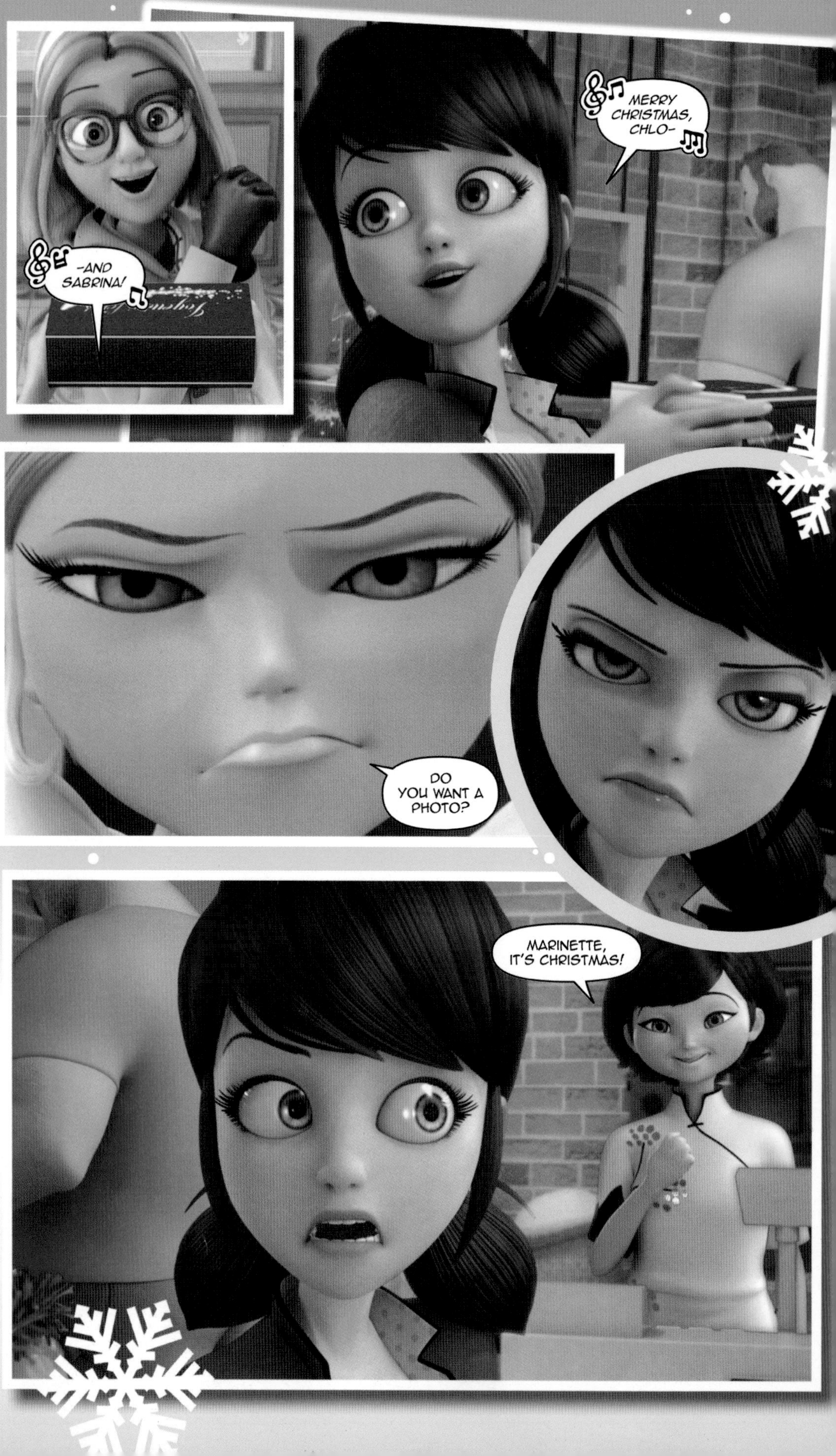
MERRY CHRISTMAS, CHLO-
-AND SABRINA!
DO YOU WANT A PHOTO?
MARINETTE, IT'S CHRISTMAS!

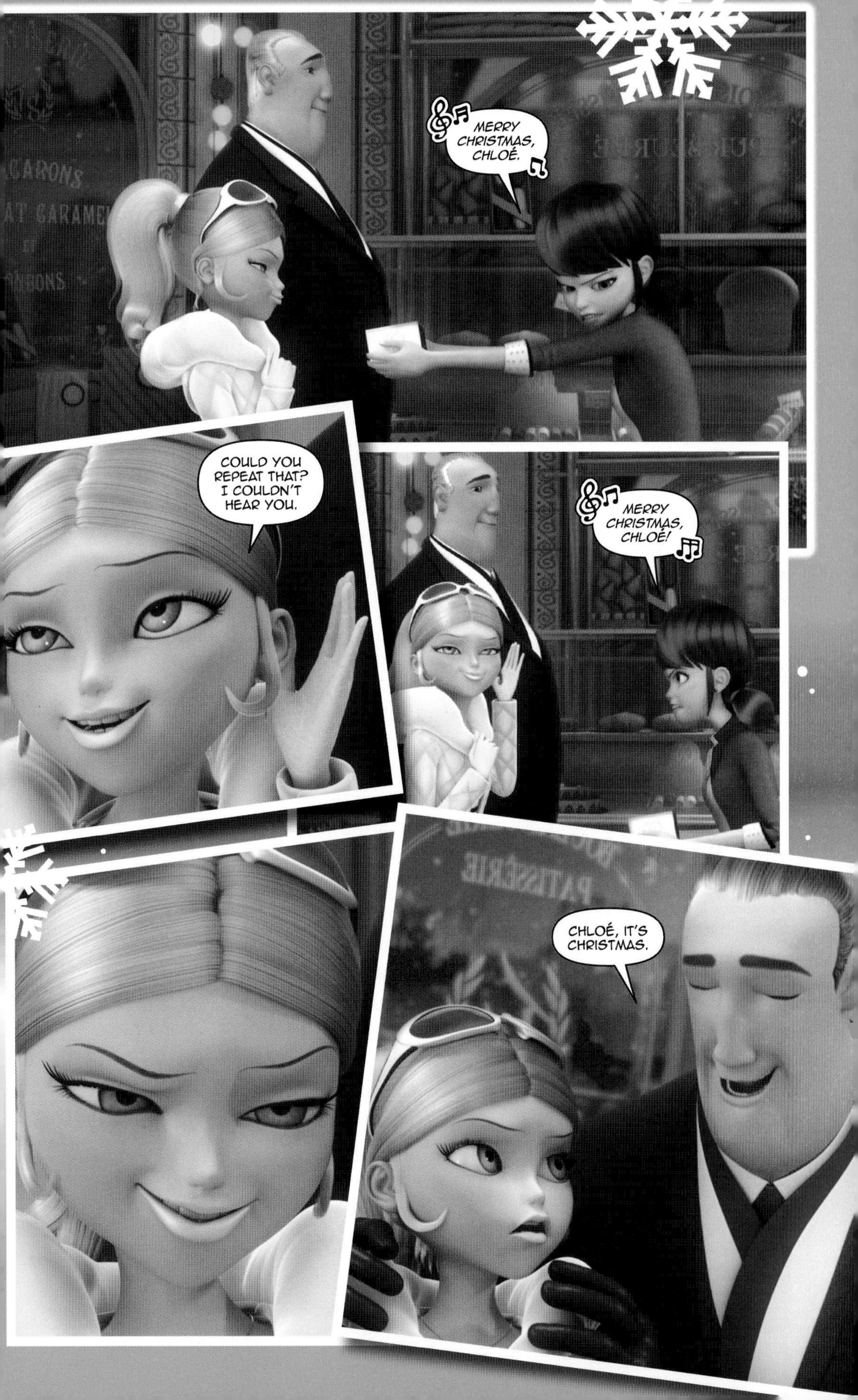

MERRY CHRISTMAS, CHLOÉ.
COULD YOU REPEAT THAT? I COULDN'T HEAR YOU.
MERRY CHRISTMAS, CHLOÉ!
CHLOÉ, IT'S CHRISTMAS.

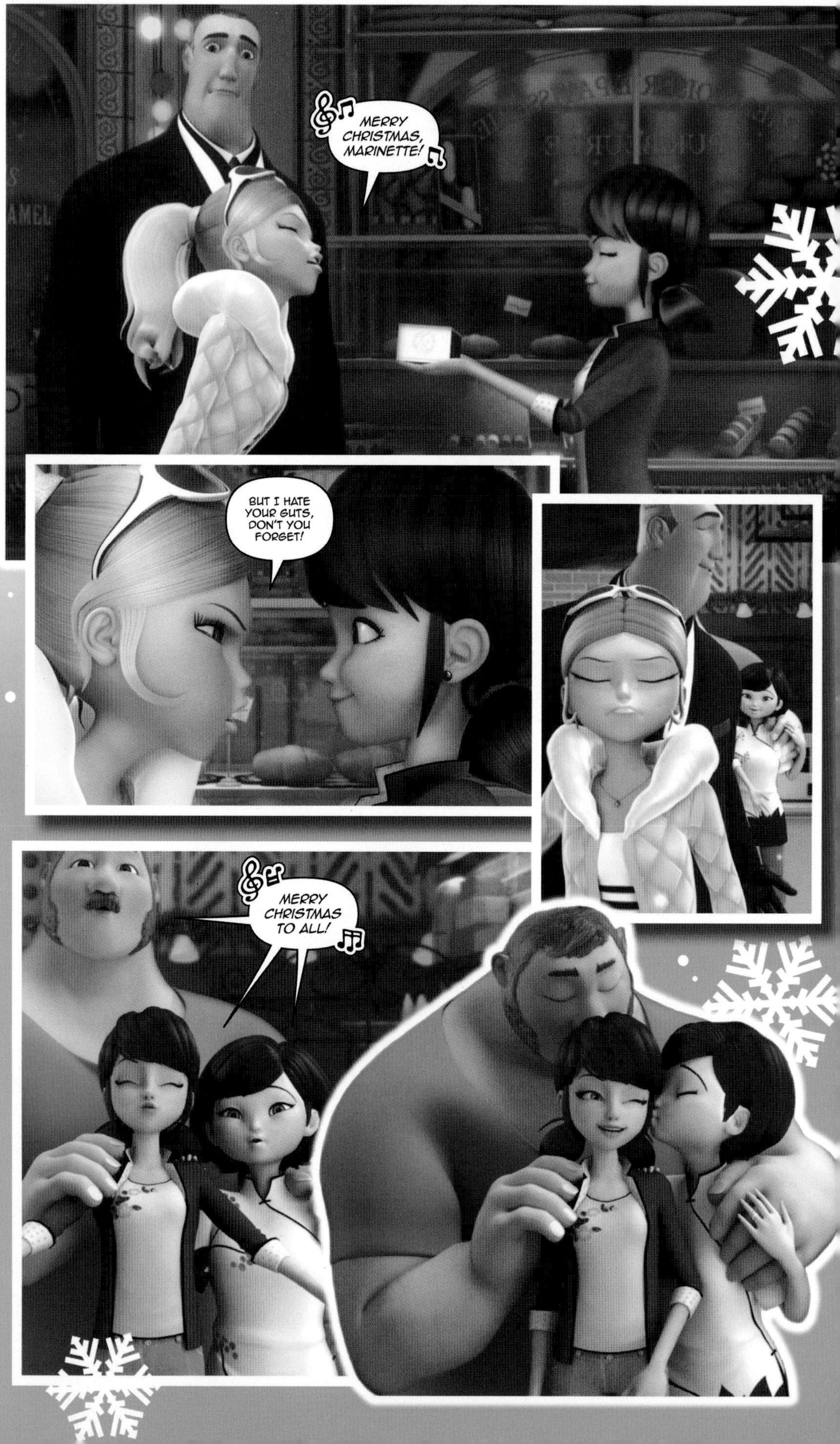
MERRY CHRISTMAS, MARINETTE!
BUT I HATE YOUR GUTS, DON'T YOU FORGET!
MERRY CHRISTMAS TO ALL!

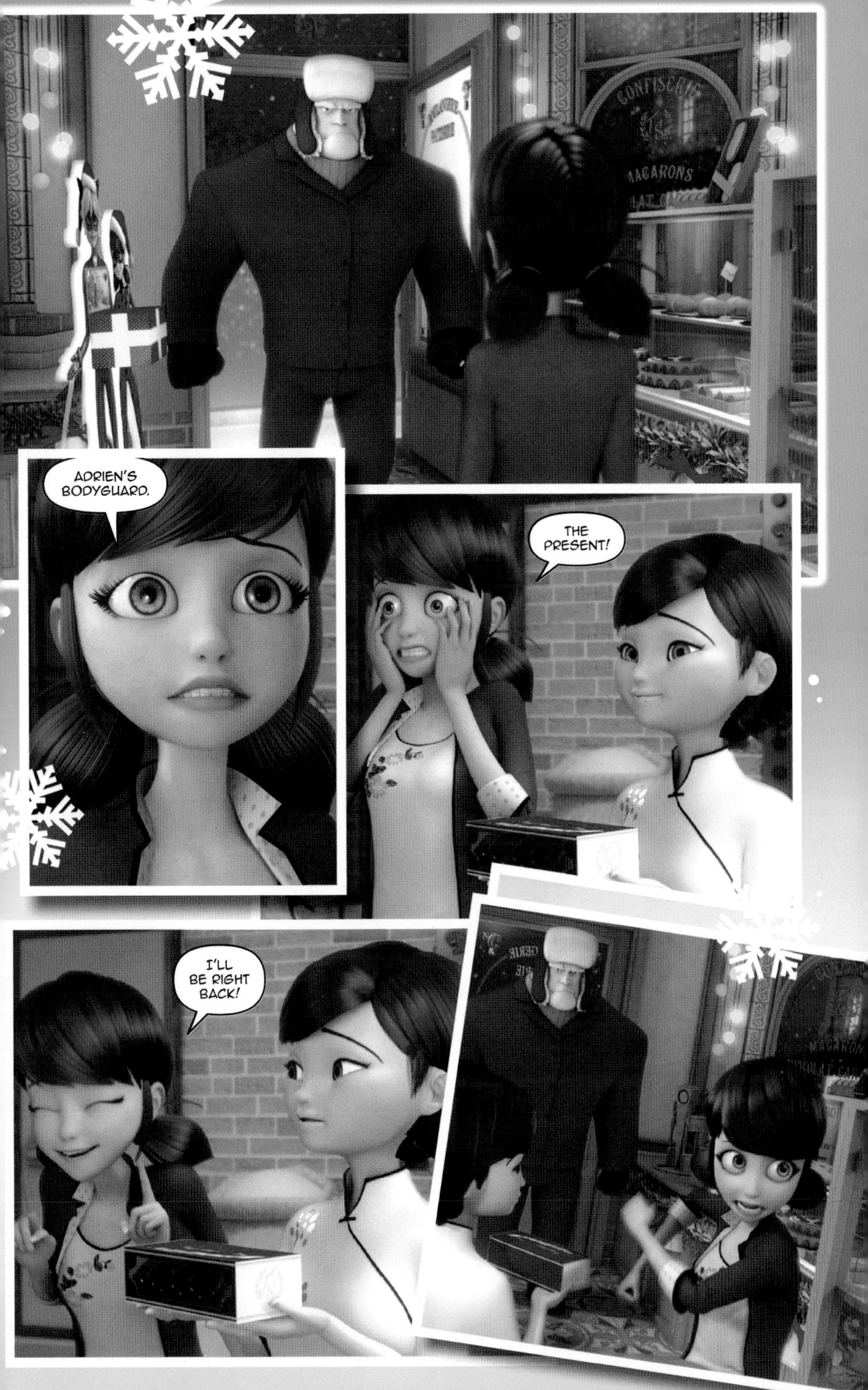
ADRIEN'S BODYGUARD.
THE PRESENT!
I'LL BE RIGHT BACK!

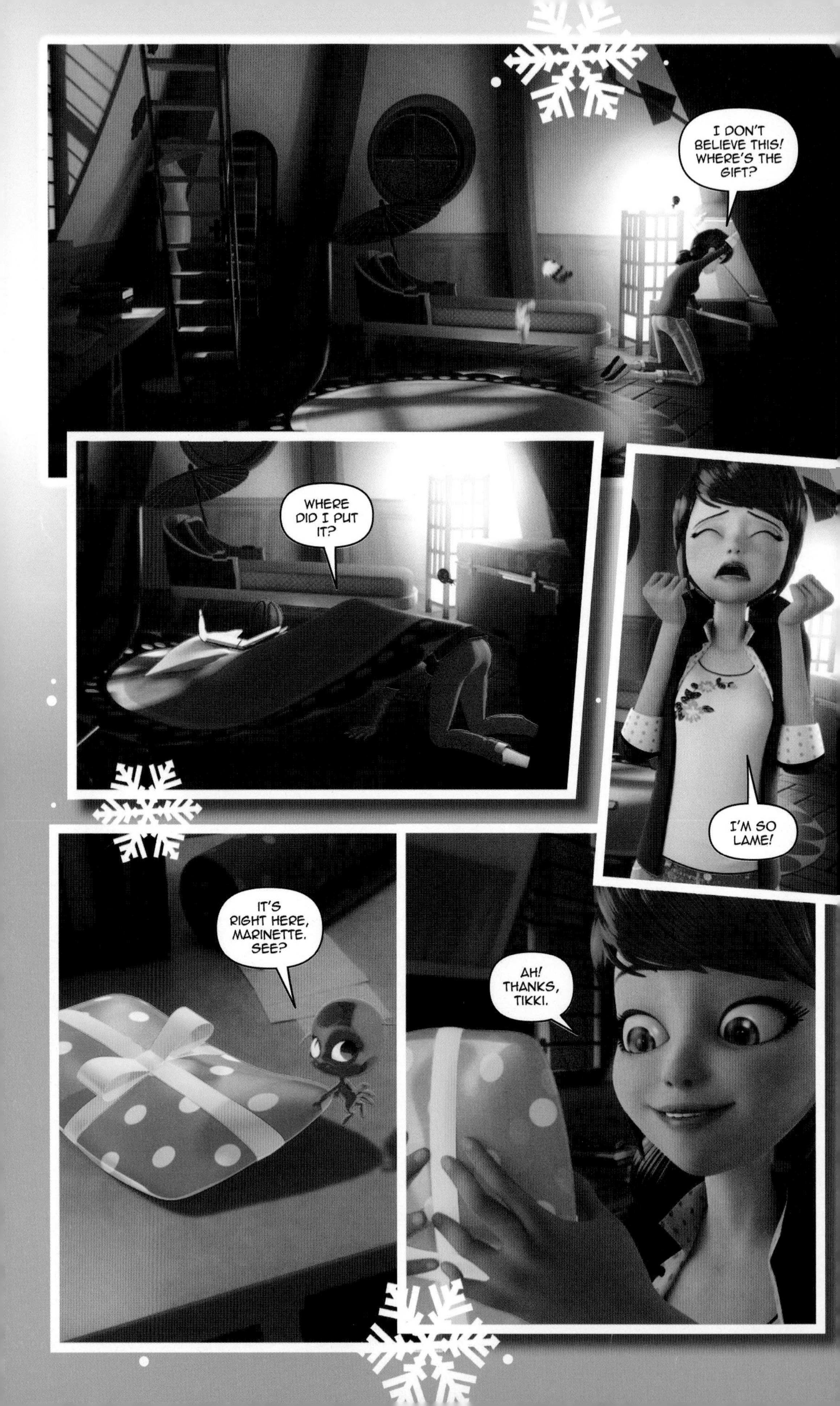
I DON'T BELIEVE THIS! WHERE'S THE GIFT?
WHERE DID I PUT IT?
I'M SO LAME!
IT'S RIGHT HERE, MARINETTE. SEE?
AH! THANKS, TIKKI.

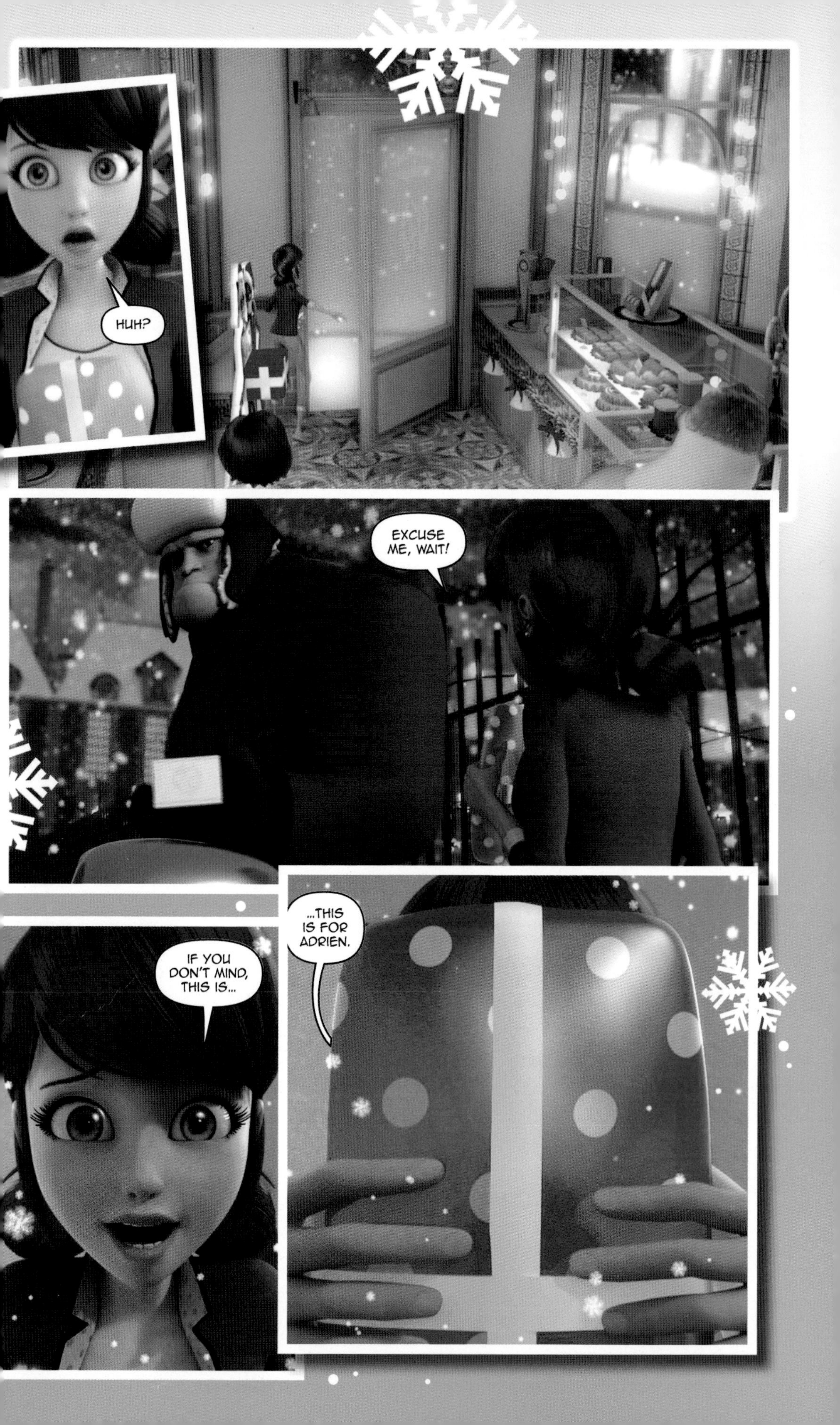
HUH?
EXCUSE ME, WAIT!
IF YOU DON'T MIND, THIS IS...
...THIS IS FOR ADRIEN.

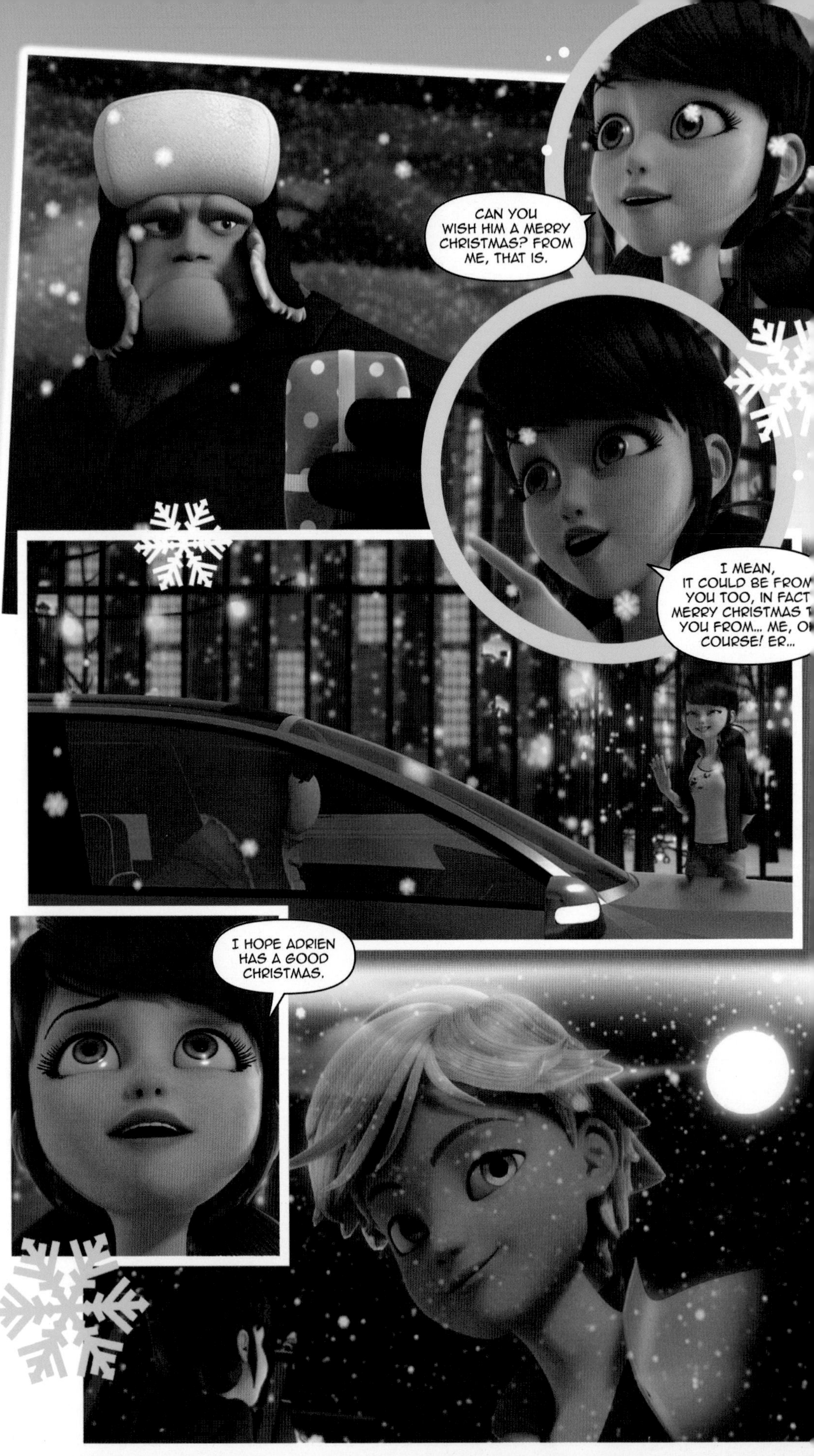
CAN YOU WISH HIM A MERRY CHRISTMAS? FROM ME, THAT IS.
I MEAN, IT COULD BE FROM YOU TOO, IN FACT MERRY CHRISTMAS T YOU FROM... ME, O COURSE! ER...
I HOPE ADRIEN HAS A GOOD CHRISTMAS.

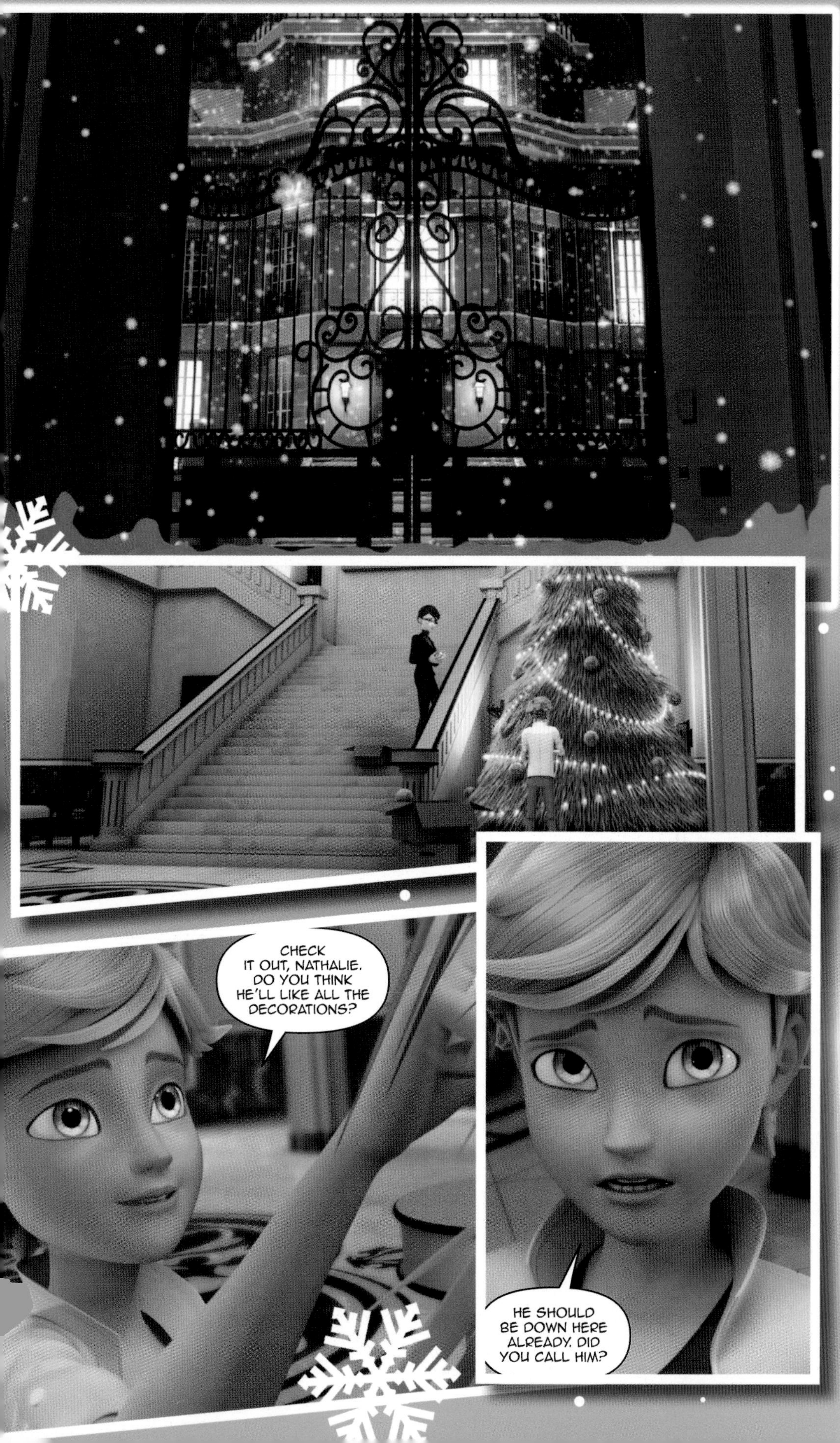
CHECK IT OUT, NATHALIE. DO YOU THINK HE'LL LIKE ALL THE DECORATIONS?
HE SHOULD BE DOWN HERE ALREADY. DID YOU CALL HIM?

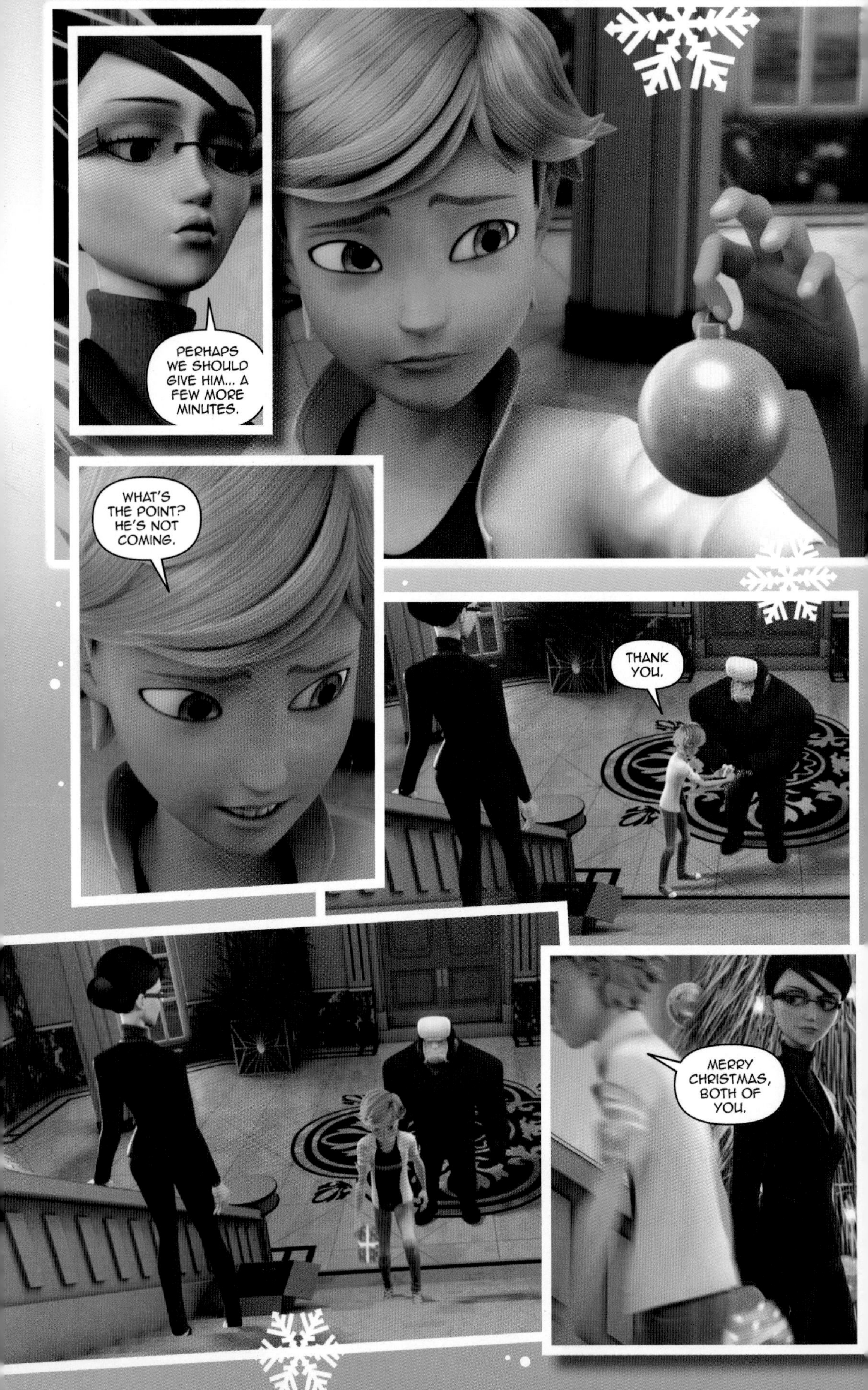
PERHAPS WE SHOULD GIVE HIM... A FEW MORE MINUTES.
WHAT'S THE POINT? HE'S NOT COMING.
THANK YOU.
MERRY CHRISTMAS, BOTH OF YOU.

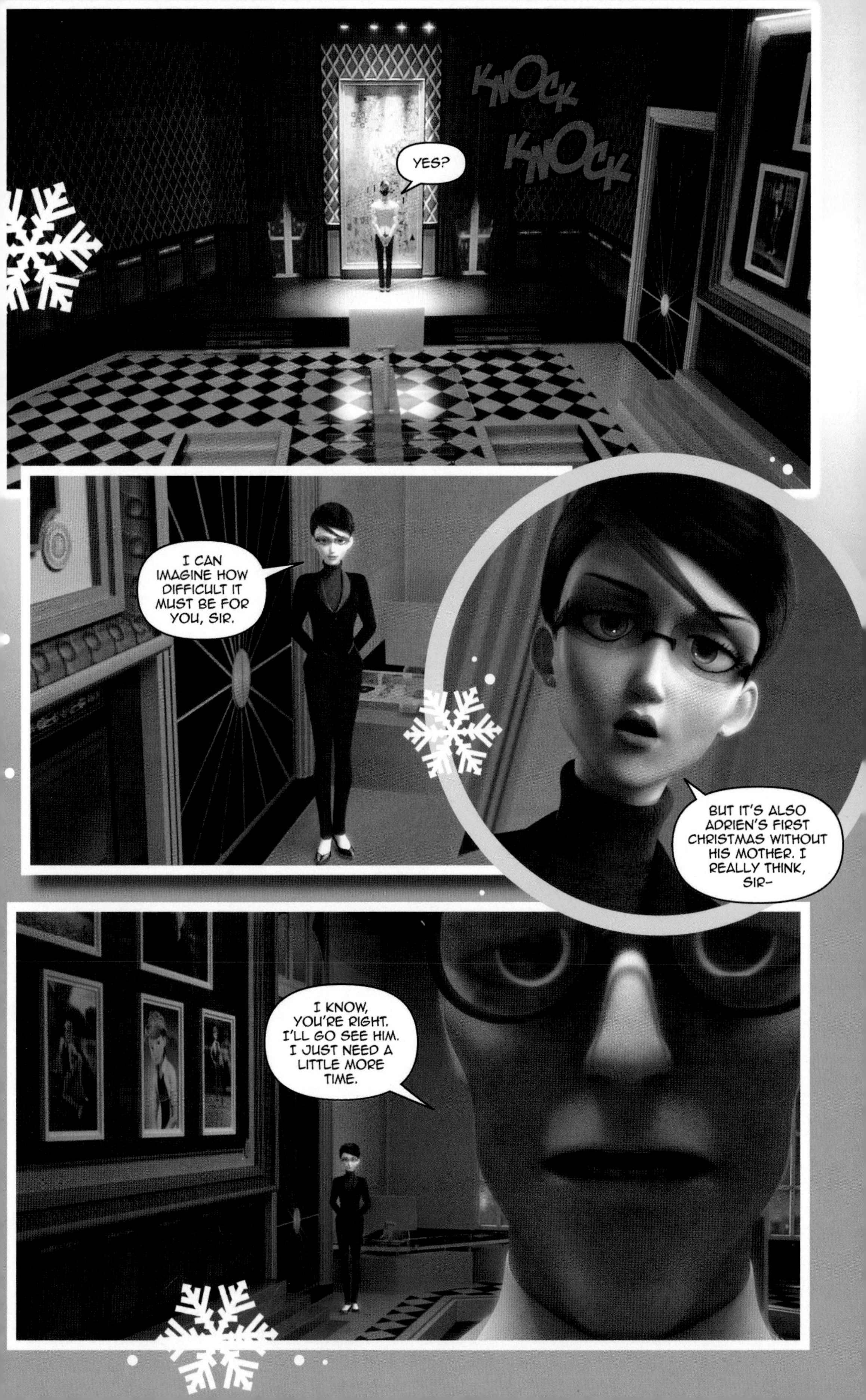
KNOCK
KNOCK
YES?
I CAN IMAGINE HOW DIFFICULT IT MUST BE FOR YOU, SIR.
BUT IT'S ALSO ADRIEN'S FIRST CHRISTMAS WITHOUT HIS MOTHER. I REALLY THINK, SIR-
I KNOW, YOU'RE RIGHT. I'LL GO SEE HIM. I JUST NEED A LITTLE MORE TIME.

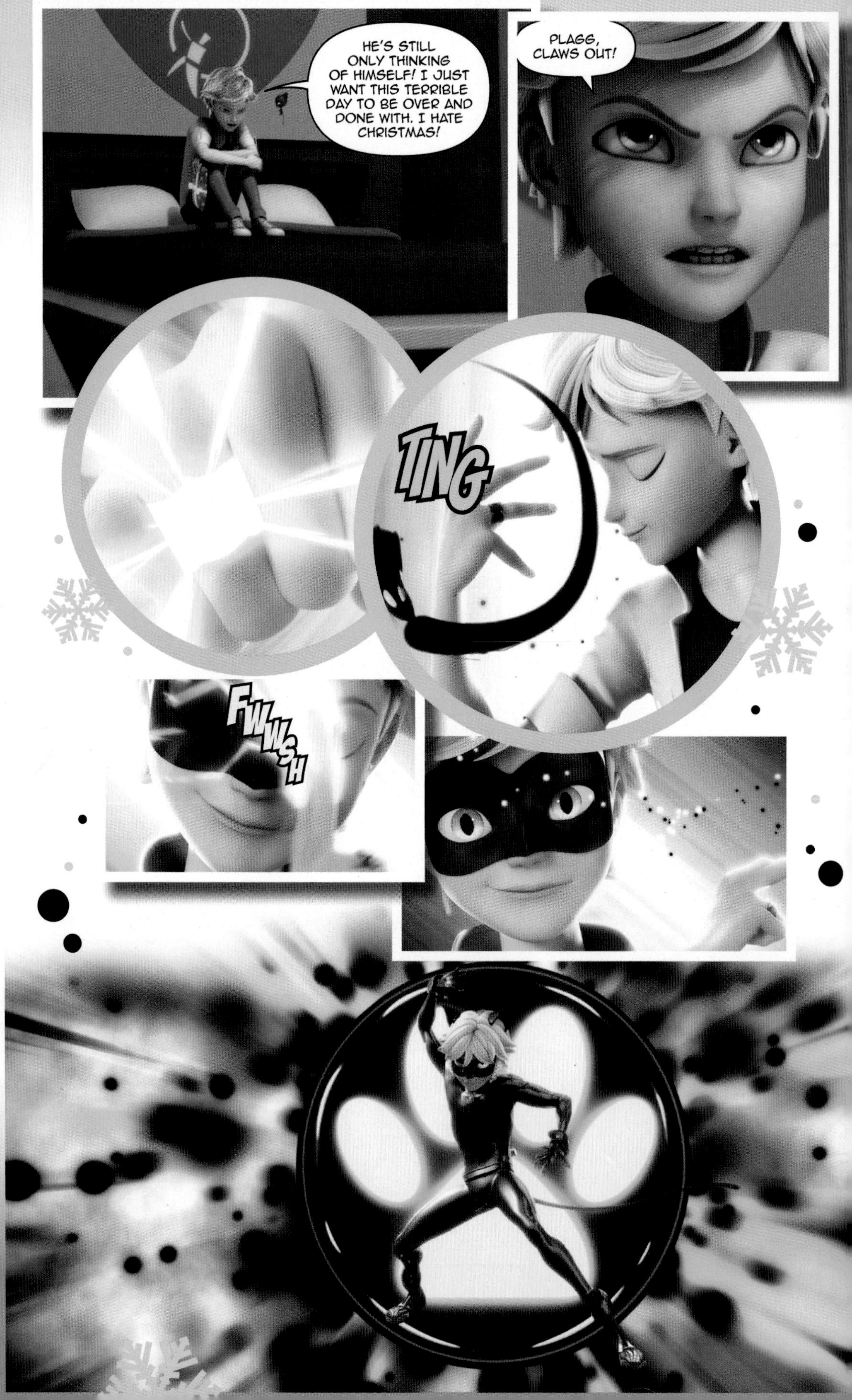
HE'S STILL ONLY THINKING OF HIMSELF! I JUST WANT THIS TERRIBLE DAY TO BE OVER AND DONE WITH. I HATE CHRISTMAS!
PLAGG, CLAWS OUT!
TING
FWWSH

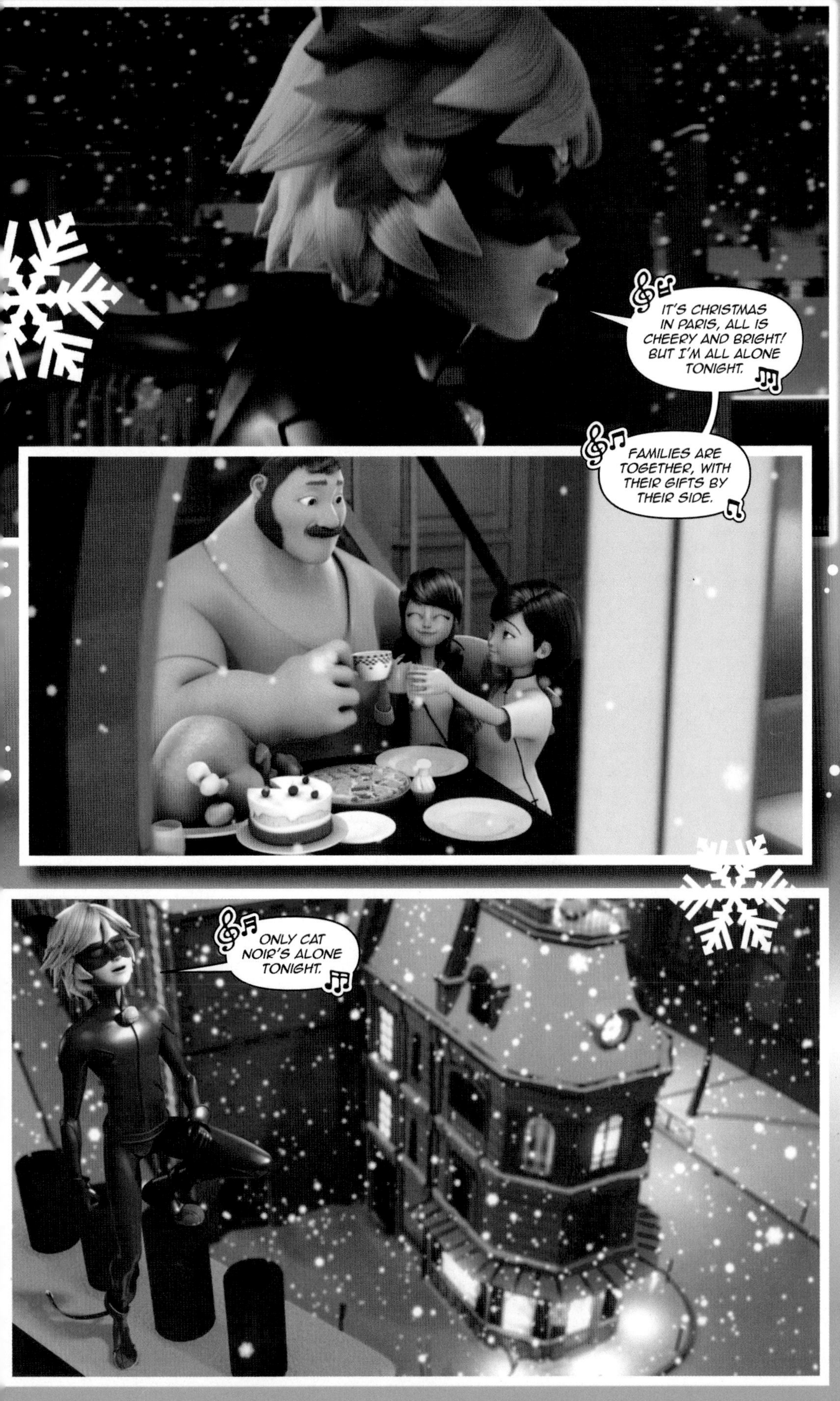
IT'S CHRISTMAS IN PARIS, ALL IS CHEERY AND BRIGHT! BUT I'M ALL ALONE TONIGHT.
FAMILIES ARE TOGETHER, WITH THEIR GIFTS BY THEIR SIDE.
ONLY CAT NOIR'S ALONE TONIGHT.

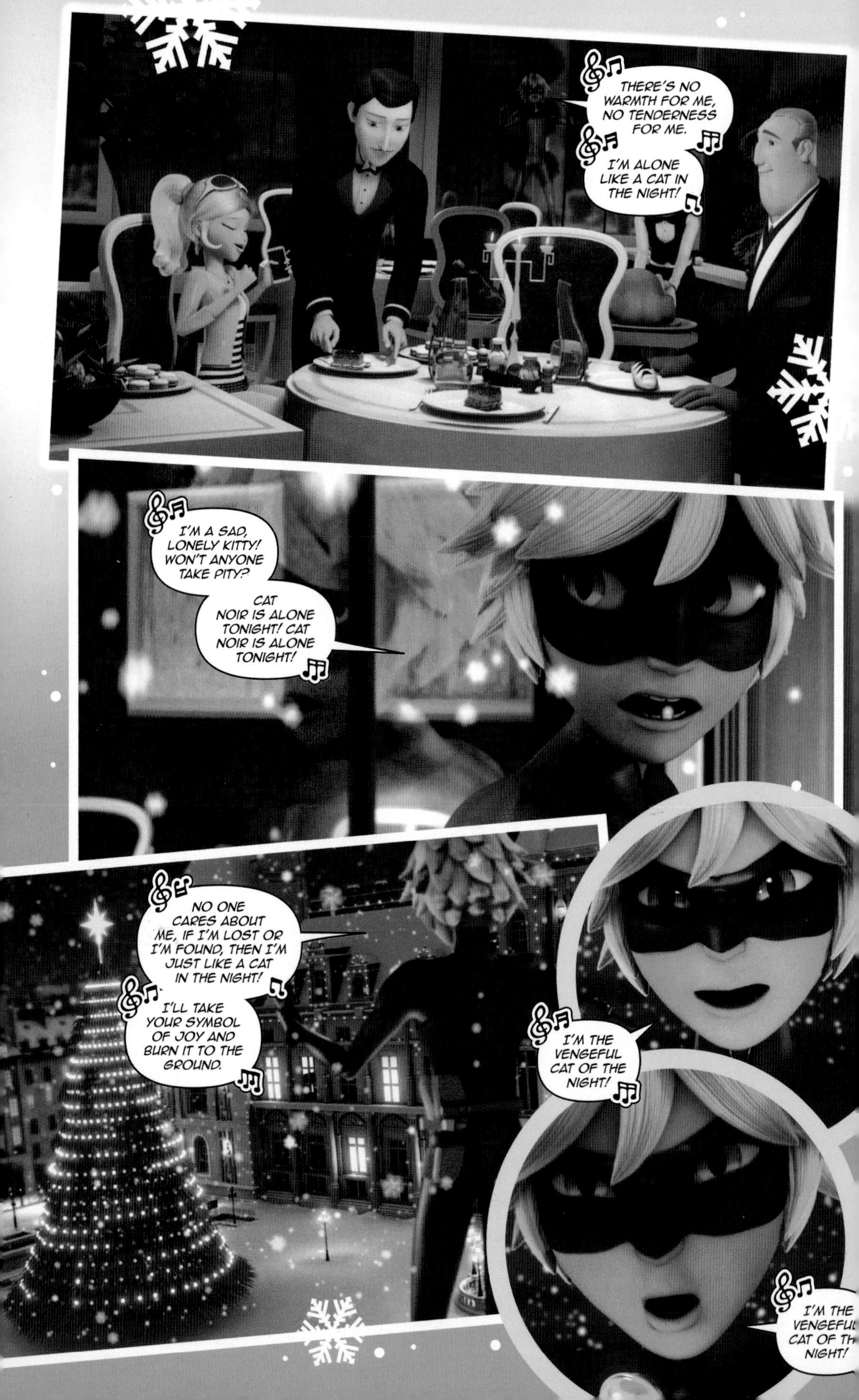
THERE'S NO WARMTH FOR ME, NO TENDERNESS FOR ME.
I'M ALONE LIKE A CAT IN THE NIGHT!
I'M A SAD, LONELY KITTY! WON'T ANYONE TAKE PITY?
CAT NOIR IS ALONE TONIGHT! CAT NOIR IS ALONE TONIGHT!
NO ONE CARES ABOUT ME, IF I'M LOST OR I'M FOUND, THEN I'M JUST LIKE A CAT IN THE NIGHT!
I'LL TAKE YOUR SYMBOL OF JOY AND BURN IT TO THE GROUND.
I'M THE VENGEFUL CAT OF THE NIGHT!

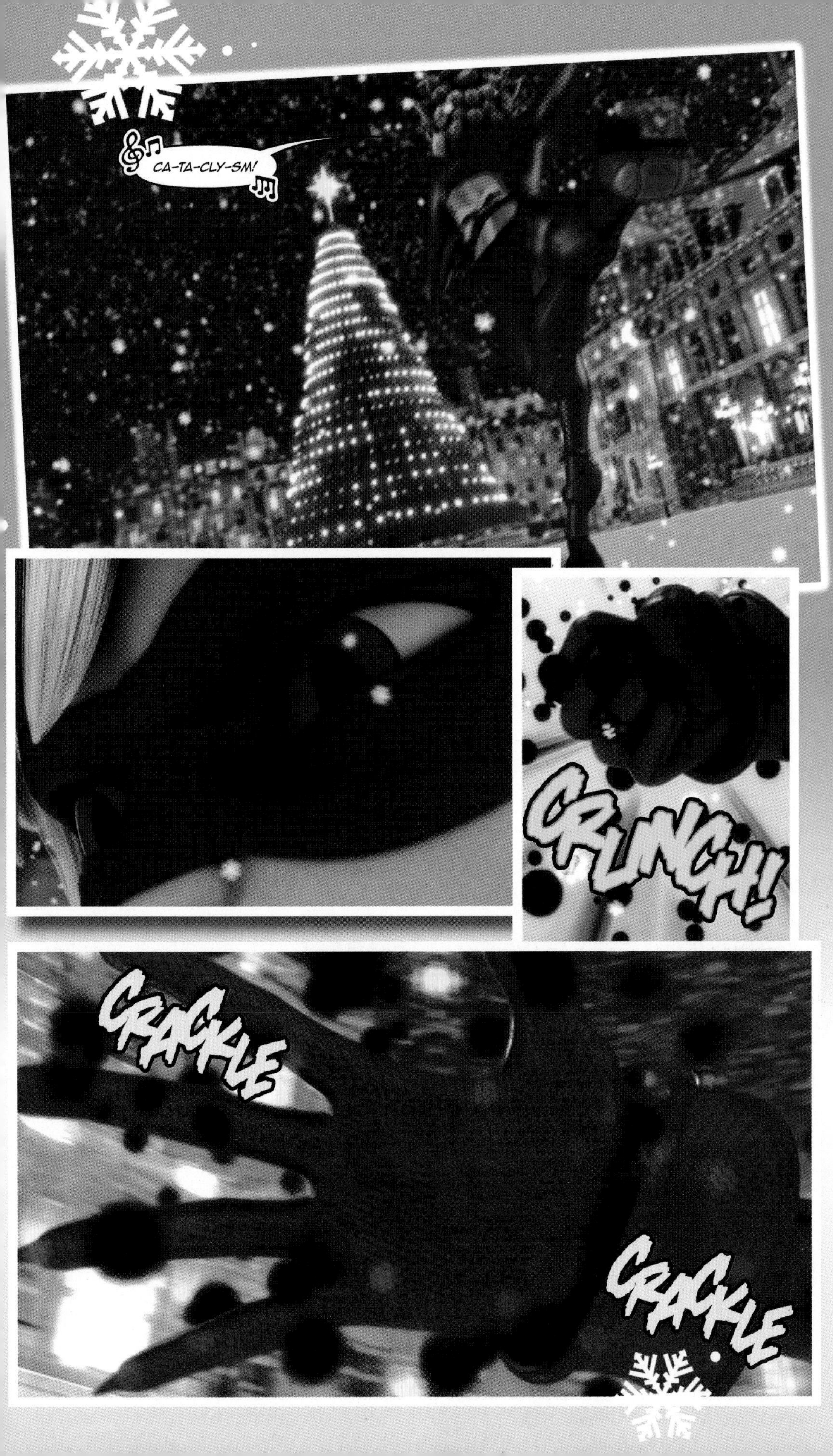

CA-TA-CLY-SM!
CRUNCH!
CRACKLE
CRACKLE

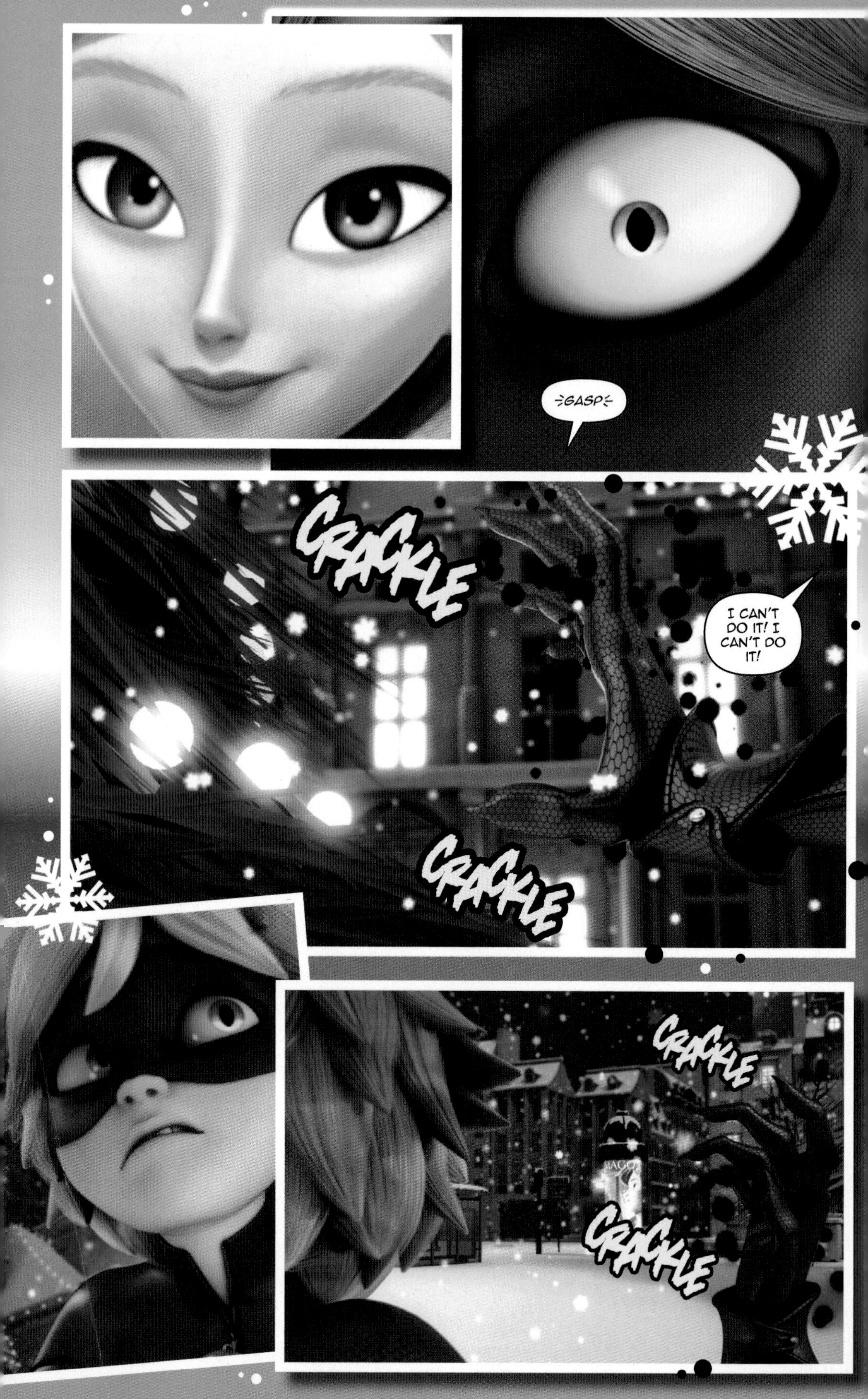
GASP
CRACKLE
I CAN'T DO IT! I CAN'T DO IT!
CRACKLE
CRACKLE
CRACKLE

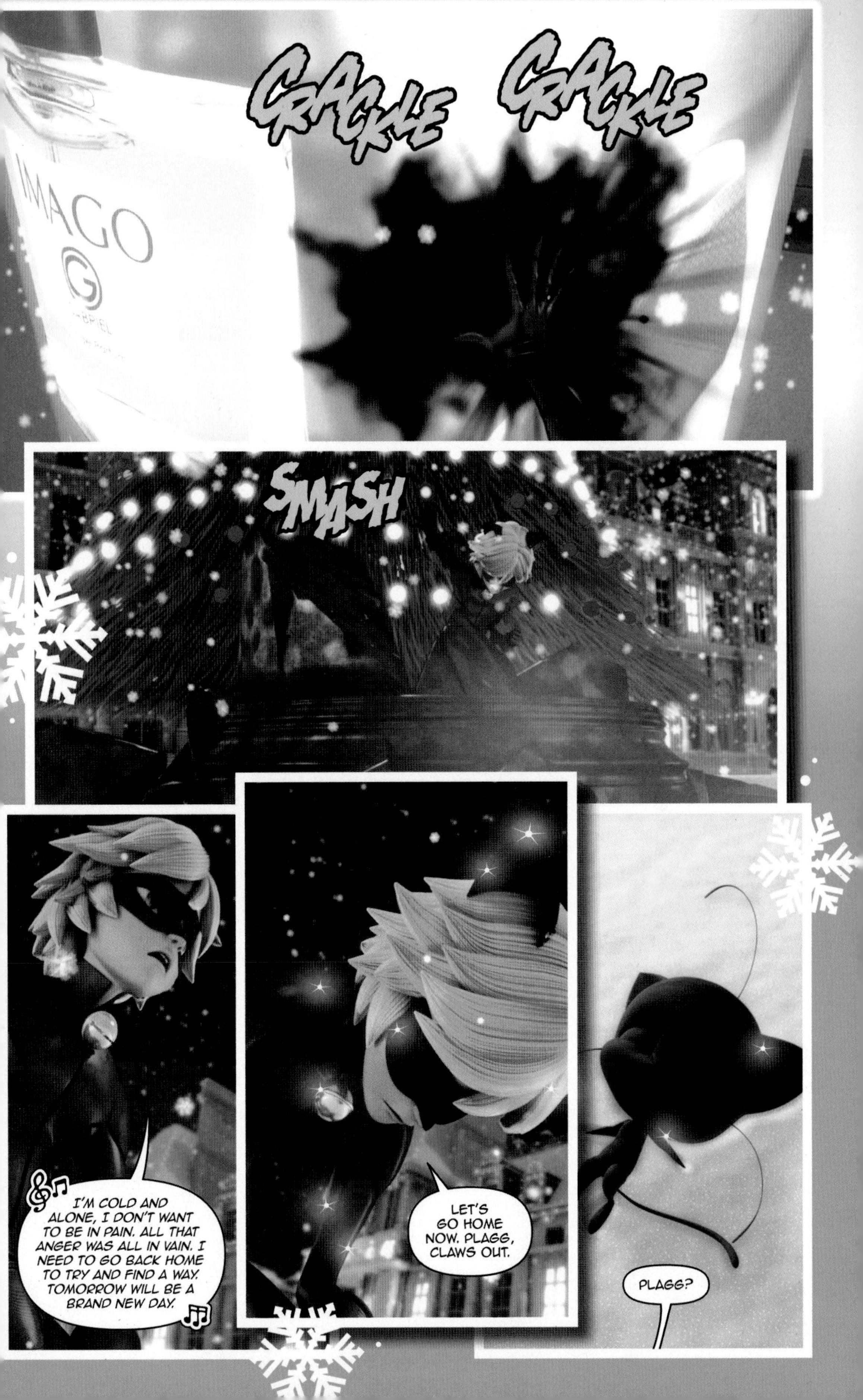
CRACKLE CRACKLE
IMAGO
SMASH
I'M COLD AND ALONE, I DON'T WANT TO BE IN PAIN. ALL THAT ANGER WAS ALL IN VAIN. I NEED TO GO BACK HOME TO TRY AND FIND A WAY. TOMORROW WILL BE A BRAND NEW DAY.
LET'S GO HOME NOW. PLAGG, CLAWS OUT.
PLAGG?

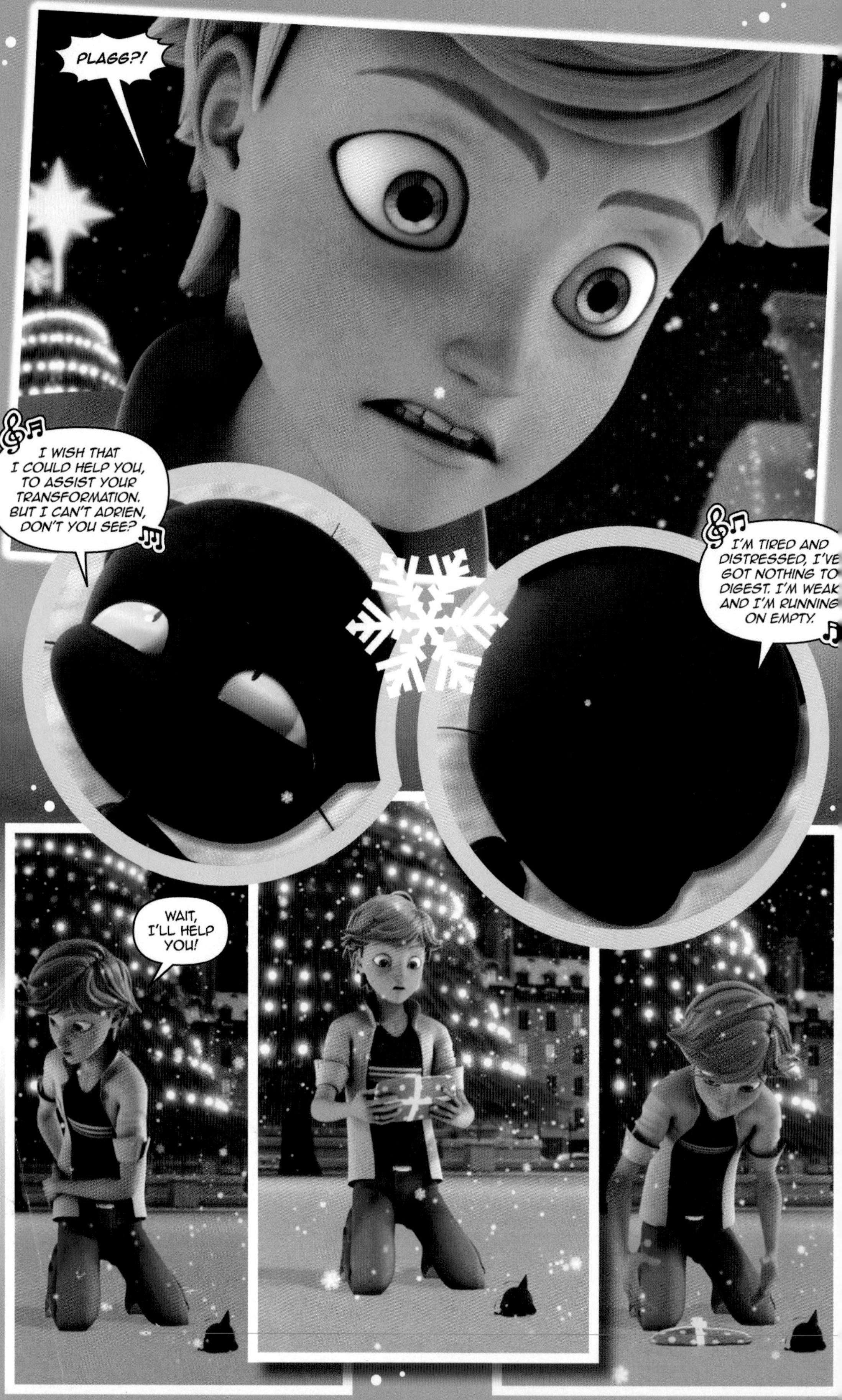
PLAGG?!
I WISH THAT I COULD HELP YOU, TO ASSIST YOUR TRANSFORMATION. BUT I CAN'T ADRIEN, DON'T YOU SEE?
I'M TIRED AND DISTRESSED, I'VE GOT NOTHING TO DIGEST. I'M WEAK AND I'M RUNNING ON EMPTY.
WAIT, I'LL HELP YOU!

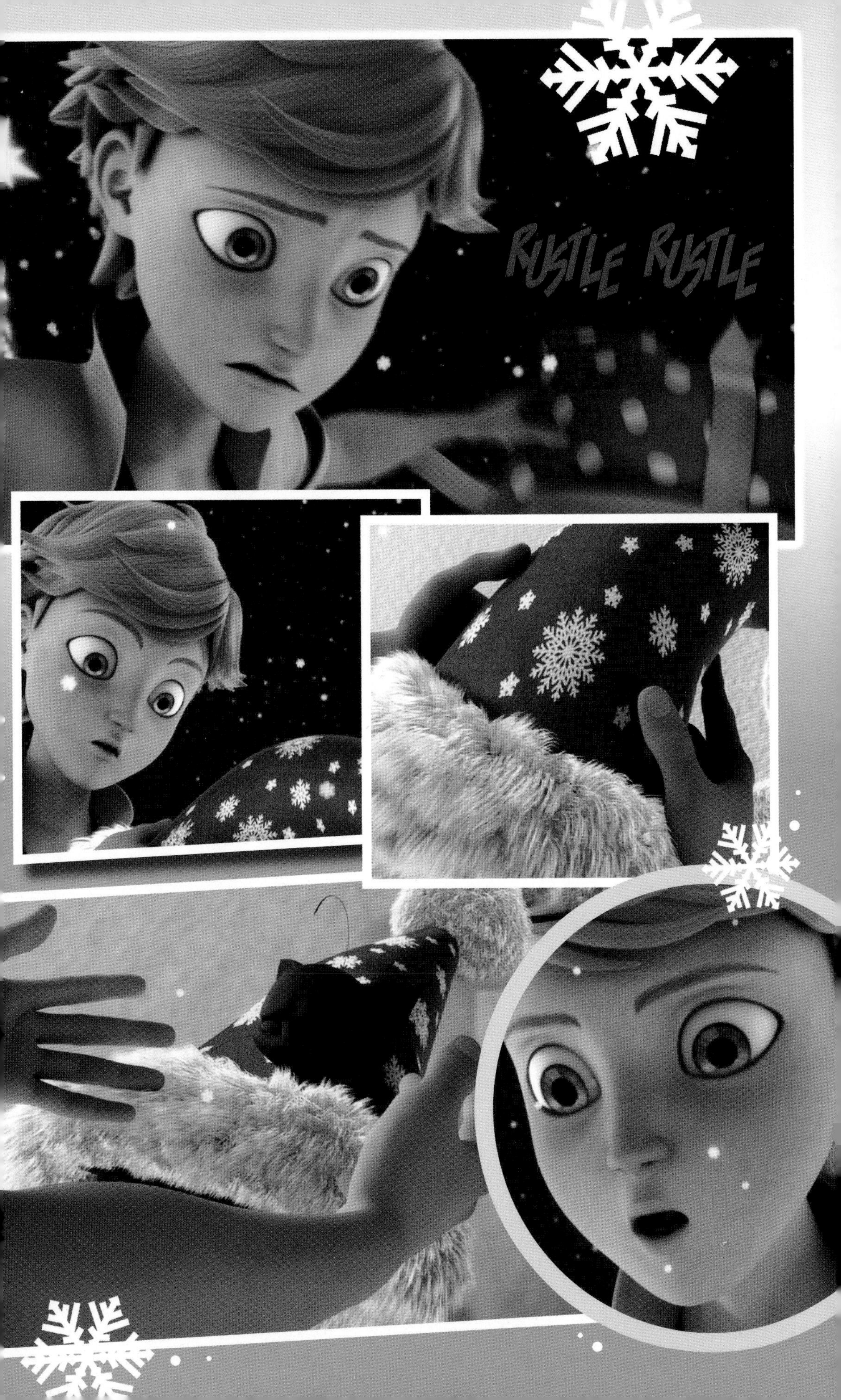
RUSTLE RUSTLE

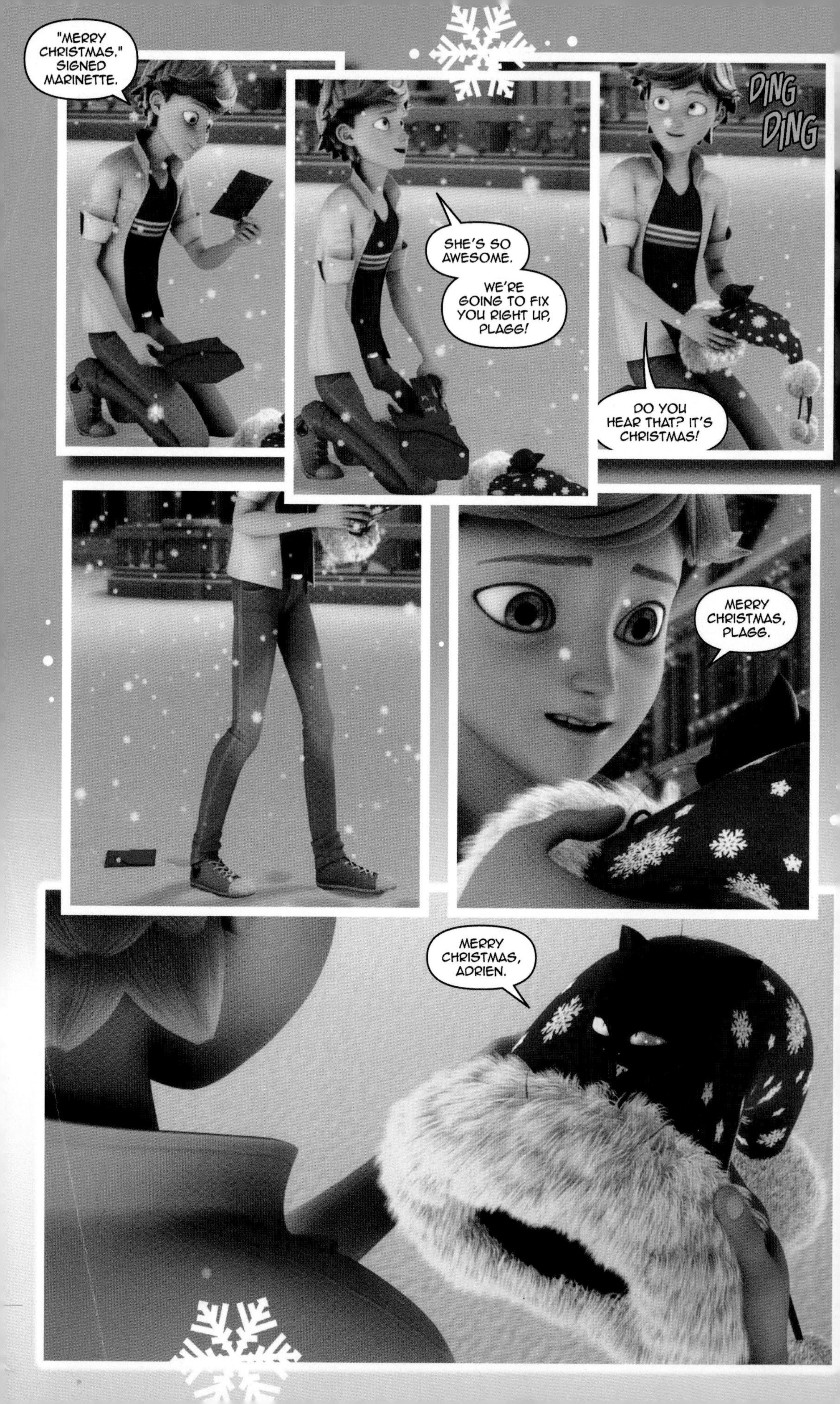
"MERRY CHRISTMAS." SIGNED MARINETTE.
SHE'S SO AWESOME.
WE'RE GOING TO FIX YOU RIGHT UP, PLAGG!
DING DING
DO YOU HEAR THAT? IT'S CHRISTMAS!
MERRY CHRISTMAS, PLAGG.
MERRY CHRISTMAS, ADRIEN.

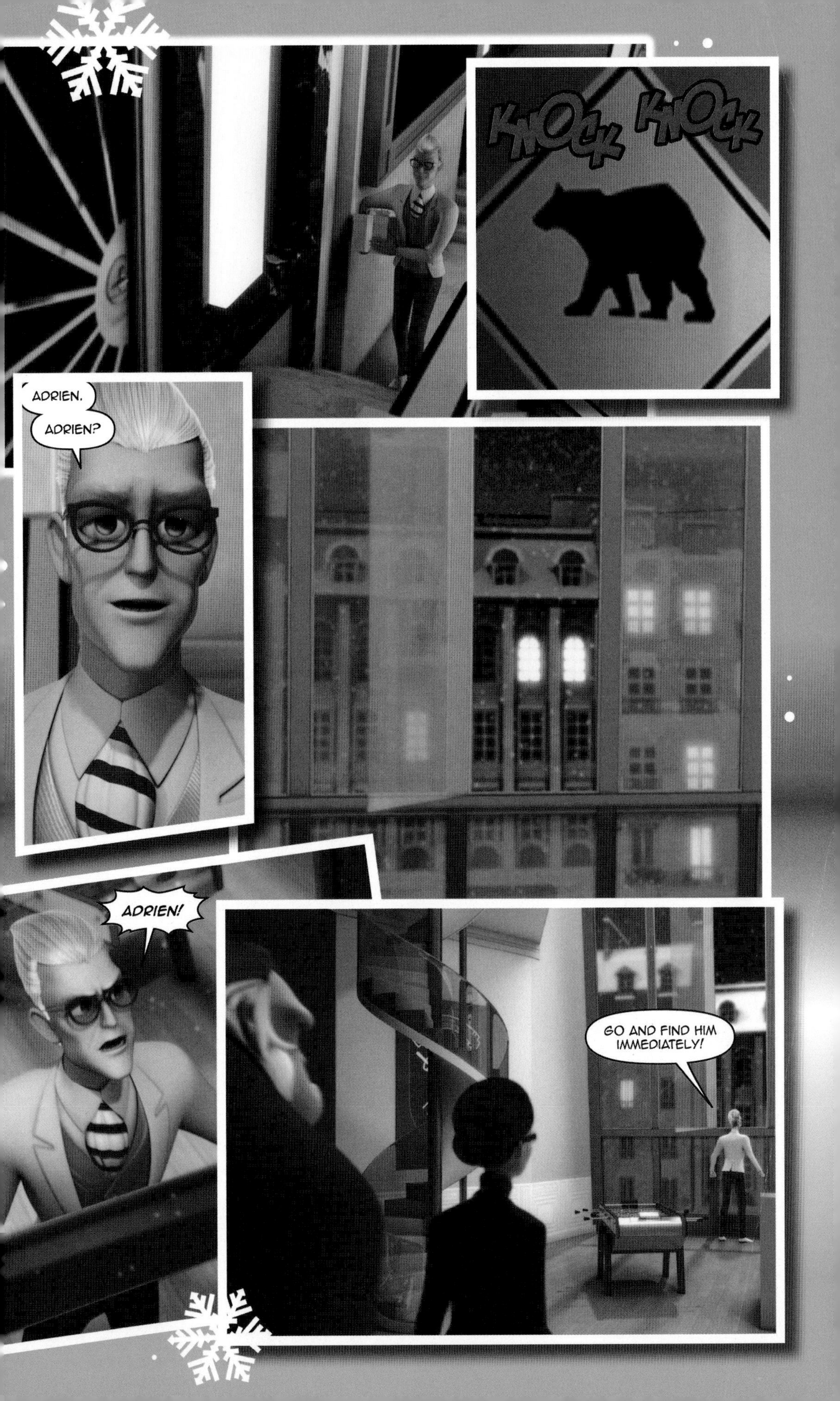
KNOCK KNOCK
ADRIEN.
ADRIEN?
ADRIEN!
GO AND FIND HIM IMMEDIATELY!

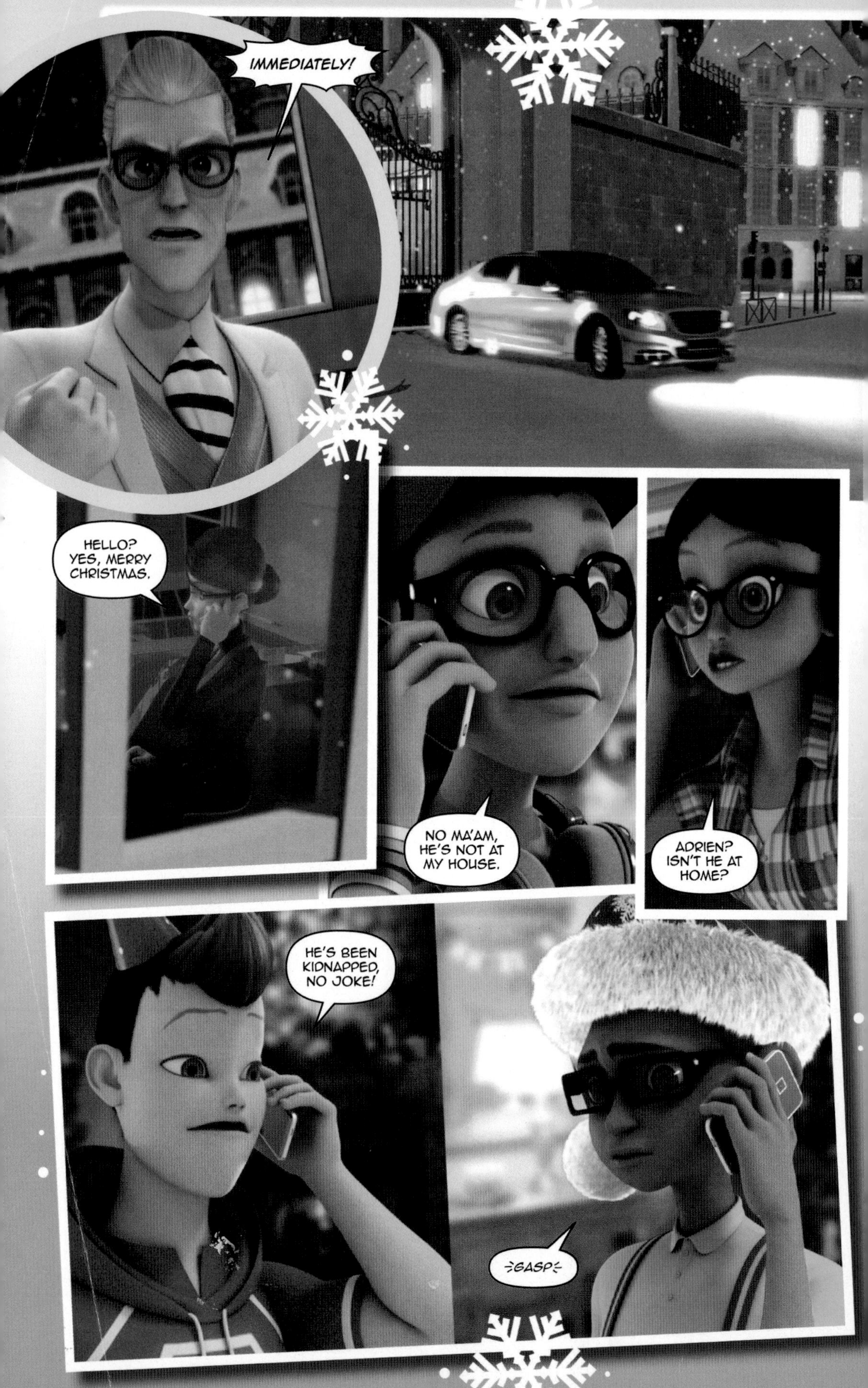
IMMEDIATELY!
HELLO? YES, MERRY CHRISTMAS.
NO MA'AM, HE'S NOT AT MY HOUSE.
ADRIEN? ISN'T HE AT HOME?
HE'S BEEN KIDNAPPED, NO JOKE!
GASP

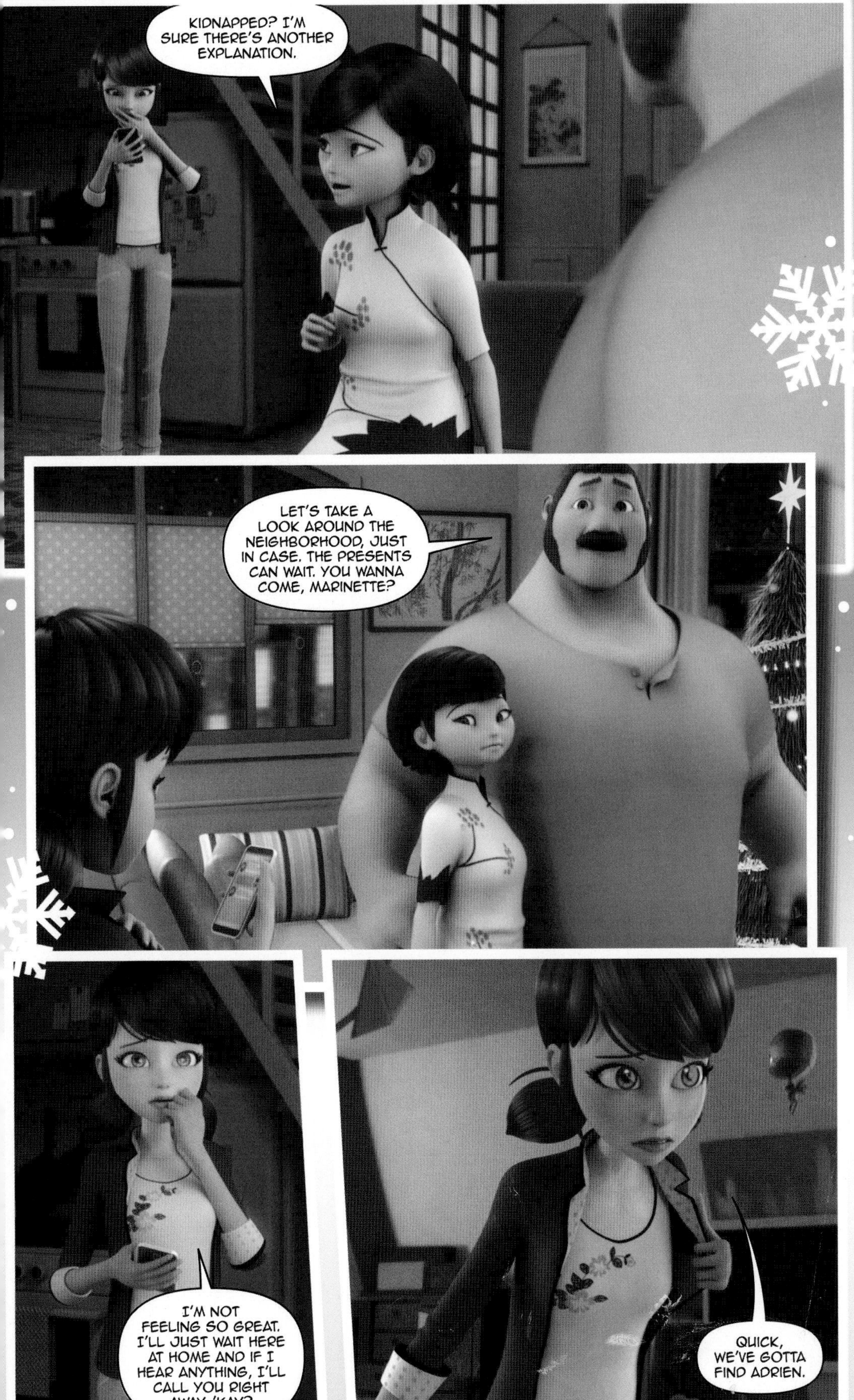
KIDNAPPED? I'M SURE THERE'S ANOTHER EXPLANATION.
LET'S TAKE A LOOK AROUND THE NEIGHBORHOOD, JUST IN CASE. THE PRESENTS CAN WAIT. YOU WANNA COME, MARINETTE?
I'M NOT FEELING SO GREAT. I'LL JUST WAIT HERE AT HOME AND IF I HEAR ANYTHING, I'LL CALL YOU RIGHT AWAY, 'KAY?
QUICK, WE'VE GOTTA FIND ADRIEN.

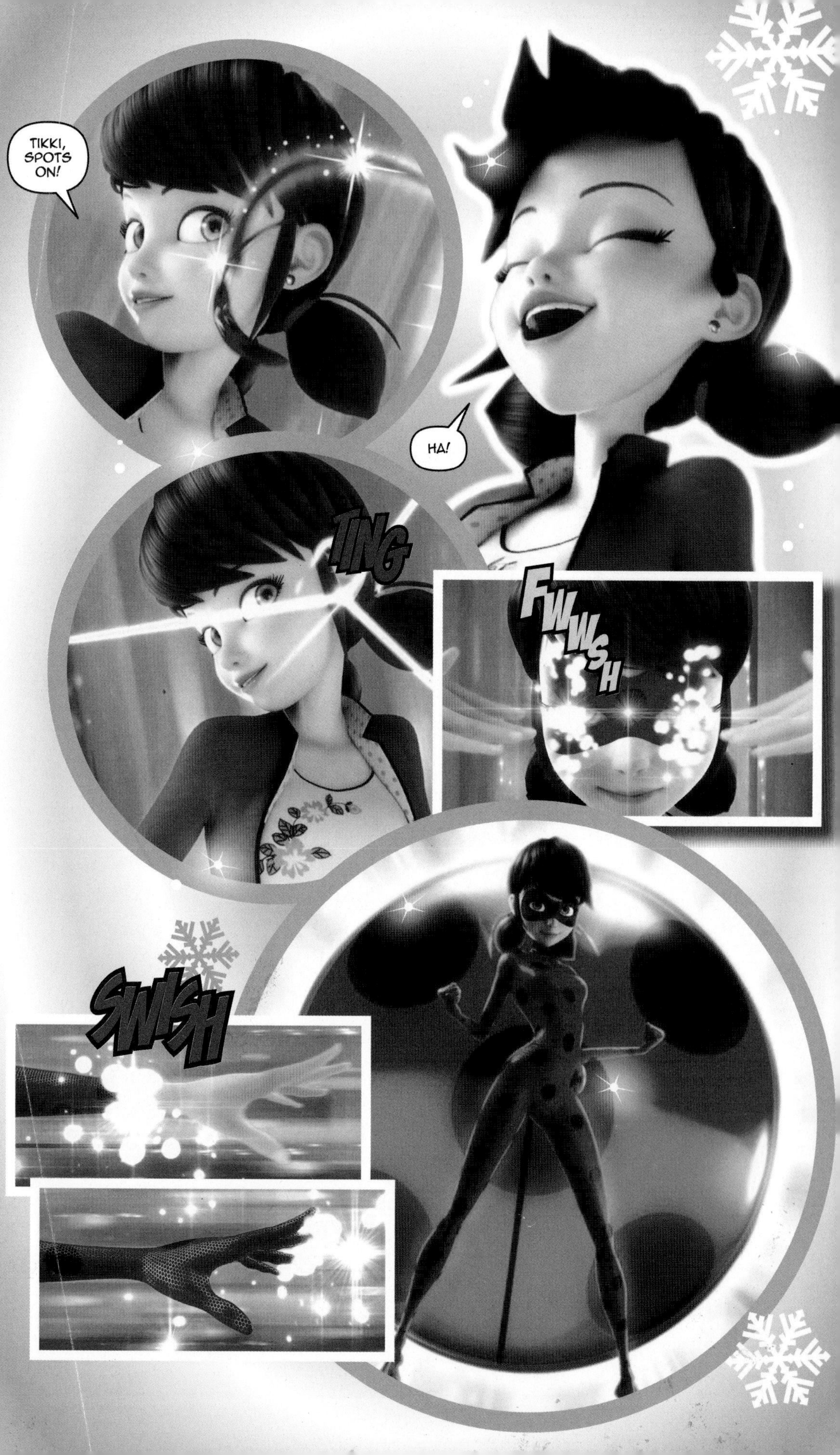
TIKKI, SPOTS ON!
HA!
TING
FWWSH
SWISH

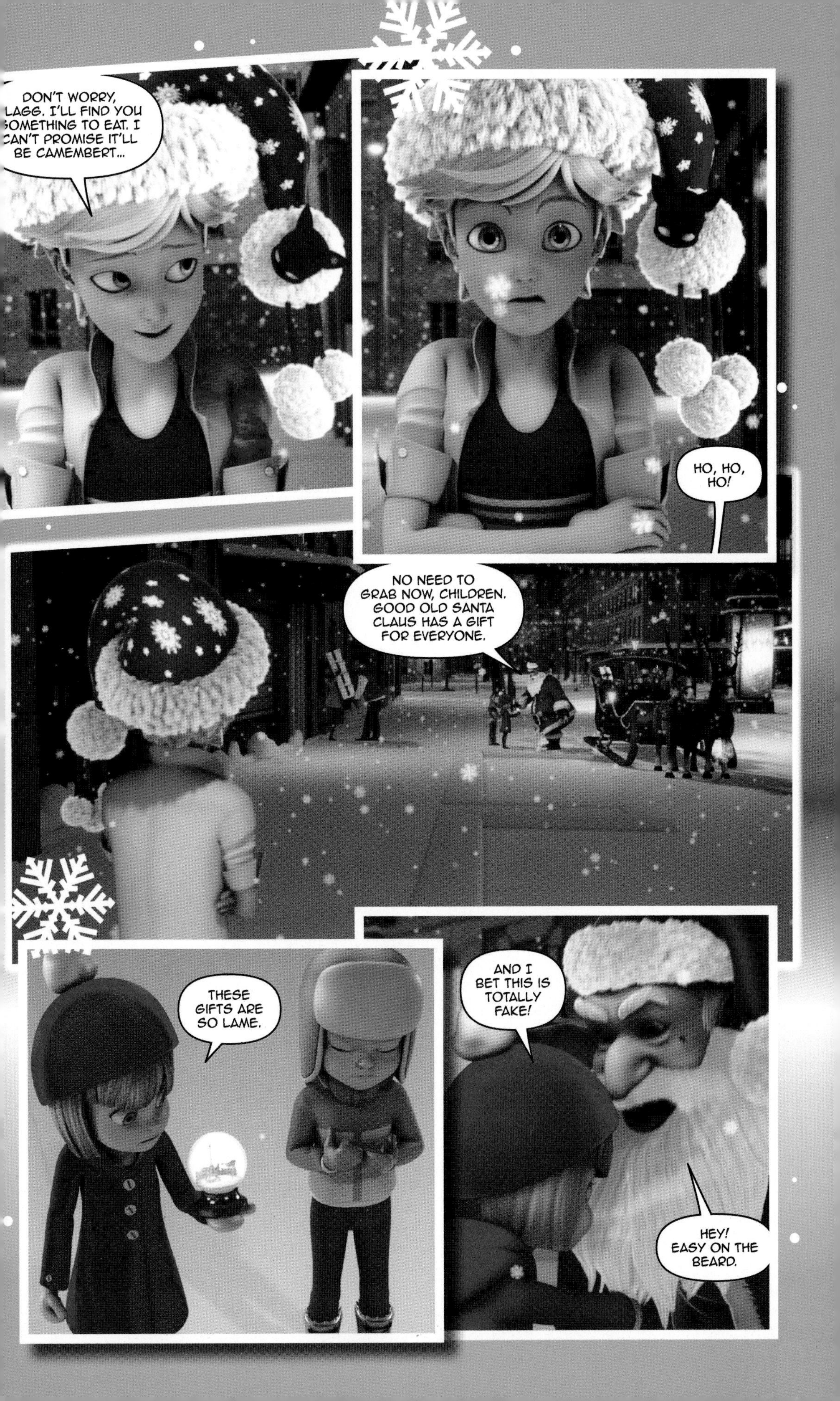
DON'T WORRY, PLAGG. I'LL FIND YOU SOMETHING TO EAT. I CAN'T PROMISE IT'LL BE CAMEMBERT...
HO, HO, HO!
NO NEED TO GRAB NOW, CHILDREN. GOOD OLD SANTA CLAUS HAS A GIFT FOR EVERYONE.
THESE GIFTS ARE SO LAME.
AND I BET THIS IS TOTALLY FAKE!
HEY! EASY ON THE BEARD.

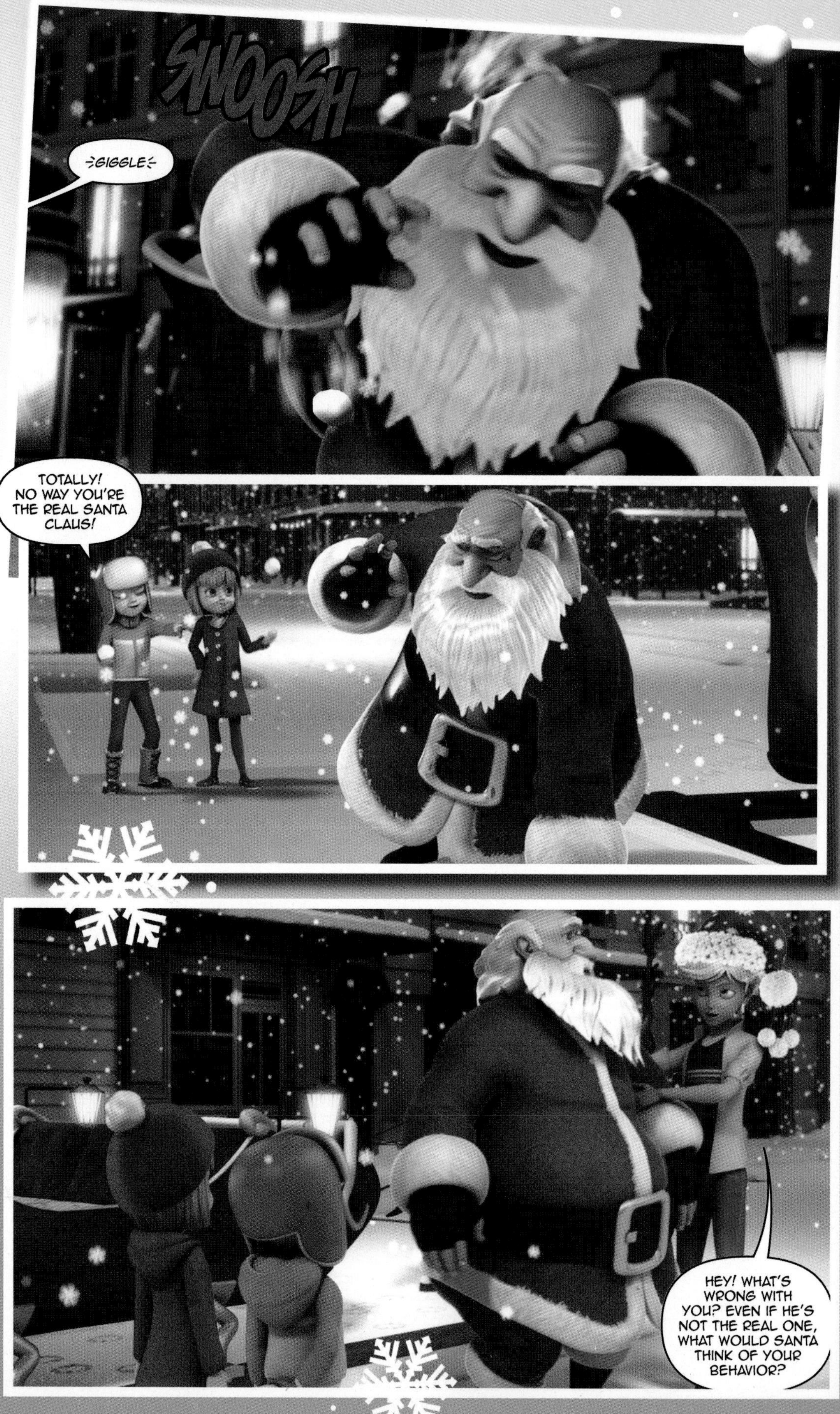
SWOOSH
GIGGLE
TOTALLY! NO WAY YOU'RE THE REAL SANTA CLAUS!
HEY! WHAT'S WRONG WITH YOU? EVEN IF HE'S NOT THE REAL ONE, WHAT WOULD SANTA THINK OF YOUR BEHAVIOR?

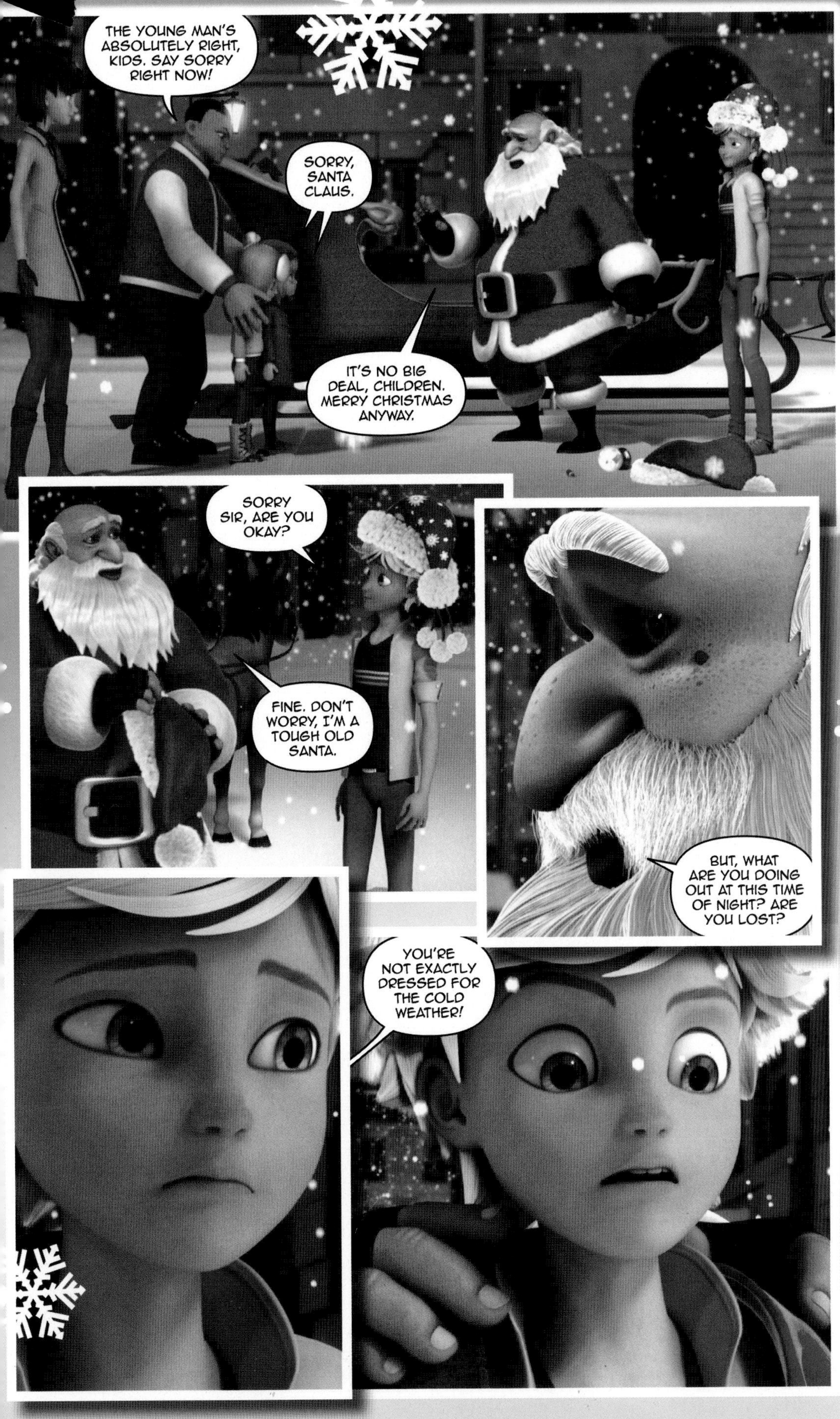
THE YOUNG MAN'S ABSOLUTELY RIGHT, KIDS. SAY SORRY RIGHT NOW!
SORRY, SANTA CLAUS.
IT'S NO BIG DEAL, CHILDREN. MERRY CHRISTMAS ANYWAY.
SORRY SIR, ARE YOU OKAY?
FINE. DON'T WORRY, I'M A TOUGH OLD SANTA.
BUT, WHAT ARE YOU DOING OUT AT THIS TIME OF NIGHT? ARE YOU LOST?
YOU'RE NOT EXACTLY DRESSED FOR THE COLD WEATHER!

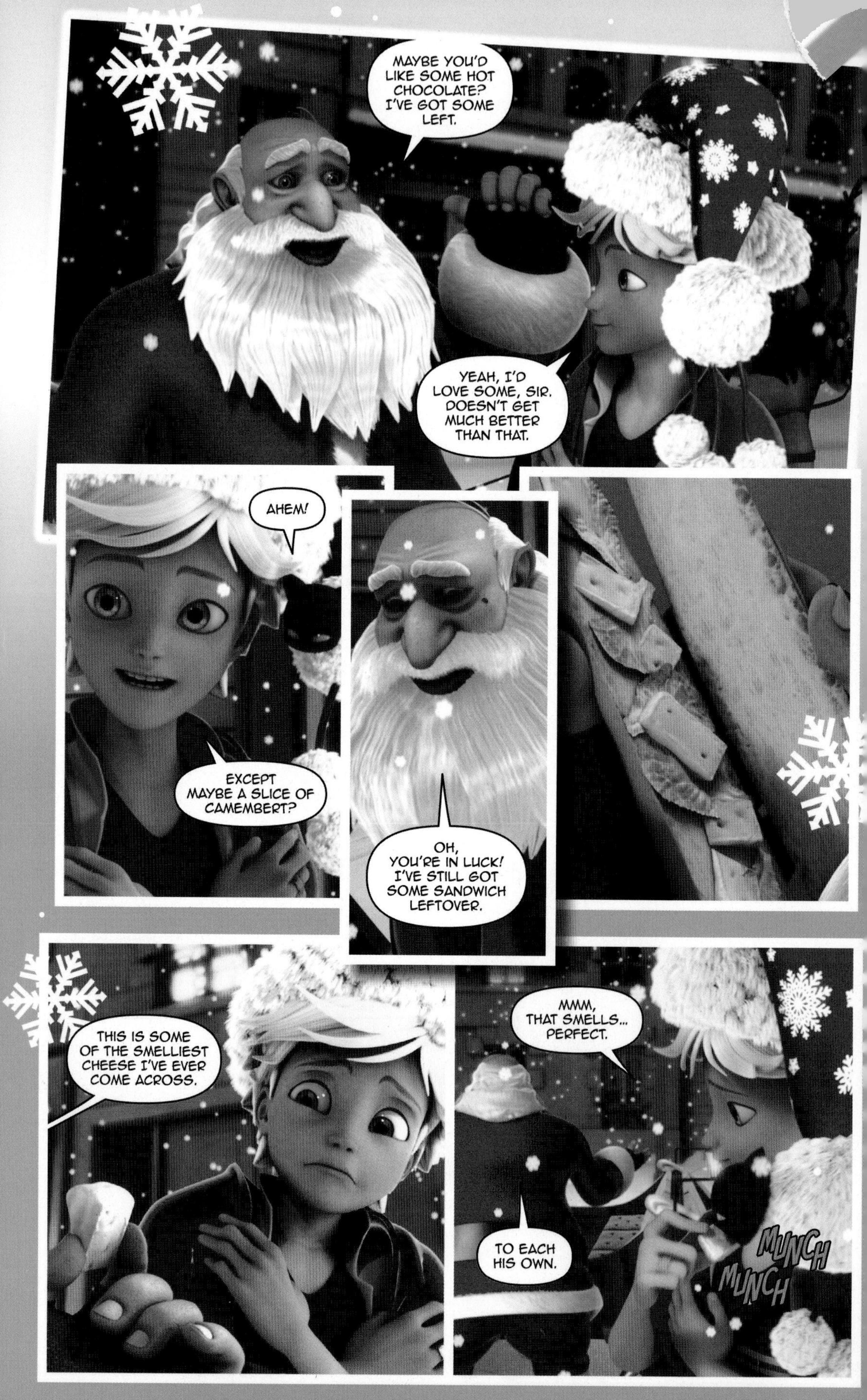
MAYBE YOU'D LIKE SOME HOT CHOCOLATE? I'VE GOT SOME LEFT.
YEAH, I'D LOVE SOME, SIR. DOESN'T GET MUCH BETTER THAN THAT.
AHEM!
EXCEPT MAYBE A SLICE OF CAMEMBERT?
OH, YOU'RE IN LUCK! I'VE STILL GOT SOME SANDWICH LEFTOVER.
THIS IS SOME OF THE SMELLIEST CHEESE I'VE EVER COME ACROSS.
MMM, THAT SMELLS... PERFECT.
TO EACH HIS OWN.
MUNCH
MUNCH

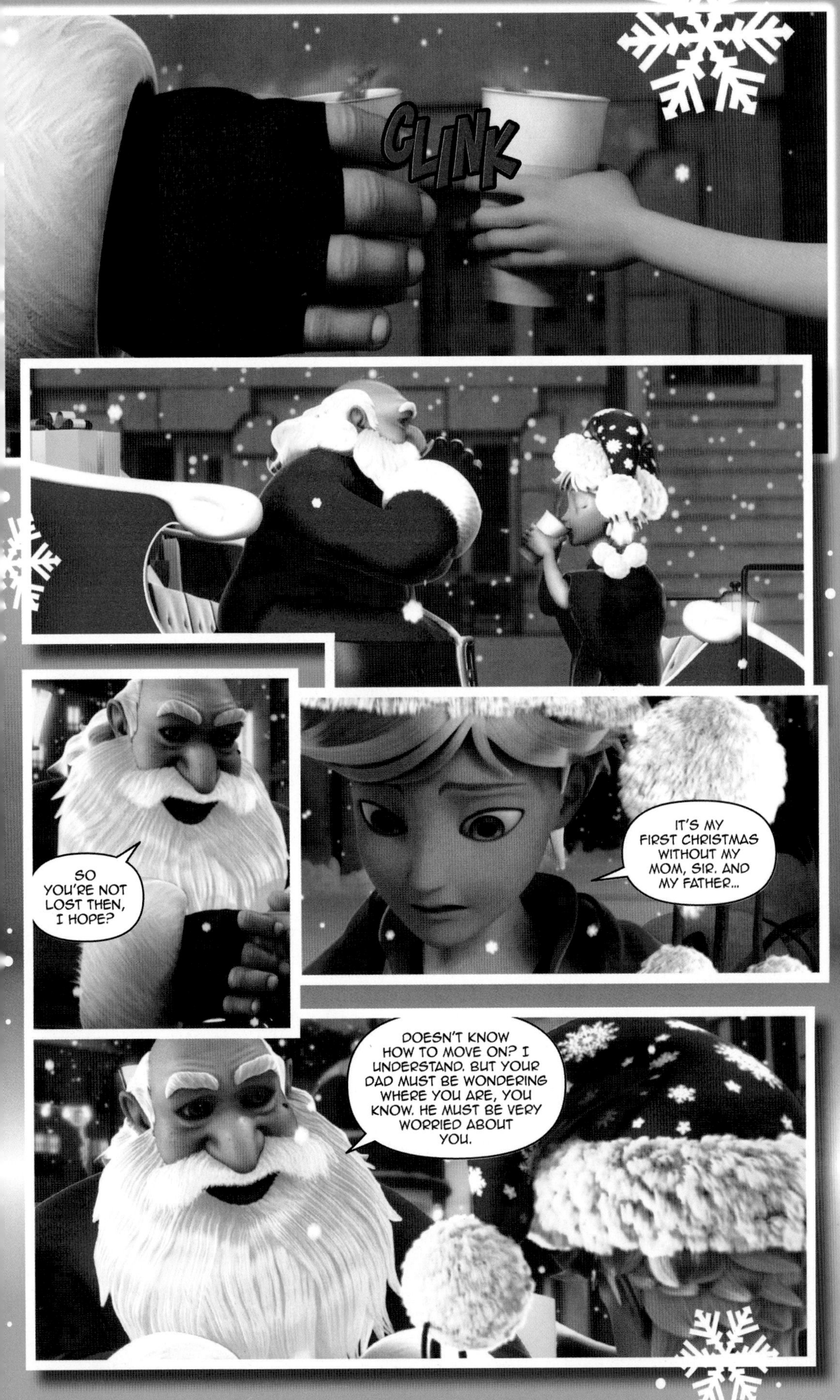

CLINK
SO YOU'RE NOT LOST THEN, I HOPE?
IT'S MY FIRST CHRISTMAS WITHOUT MY MOM, SIR. AND MY FATHER...
DOESN'T KNOW HOW TO MOVE ON? I UNDERSTAND. BUT YOUR DAD MUST BE WONDERING WHERE YOU ARE, YOU KNOW. HE MUST BE VERY WORRIED ABOUT YOU.

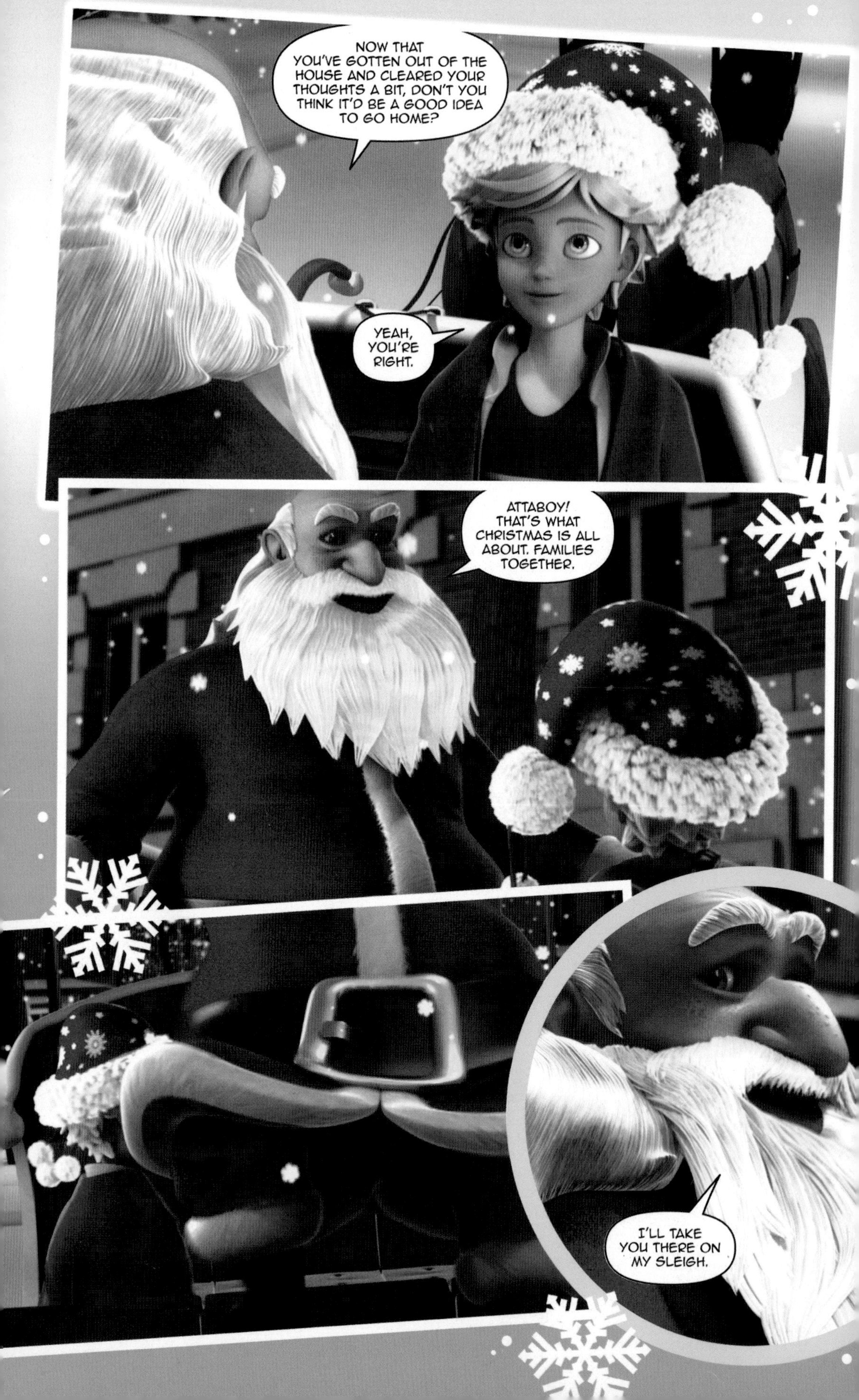
NOW THAT YOU'VE GOTTEN OUT OF THE HOUSE AND CLEARED YOUR THOUGHTS A BIT, DON'T YOU THINK IT'D BE A GOOD IDEA TO GO HOME?
YEAH, YOU'RE RIGHT.
ATTABOY! THAT'S WHAT CHRISTMAS IS ALL ABOUT. FAMILIES TOGETHER.
I'LL TAKE YOU THERE ON MY SLEIGH.

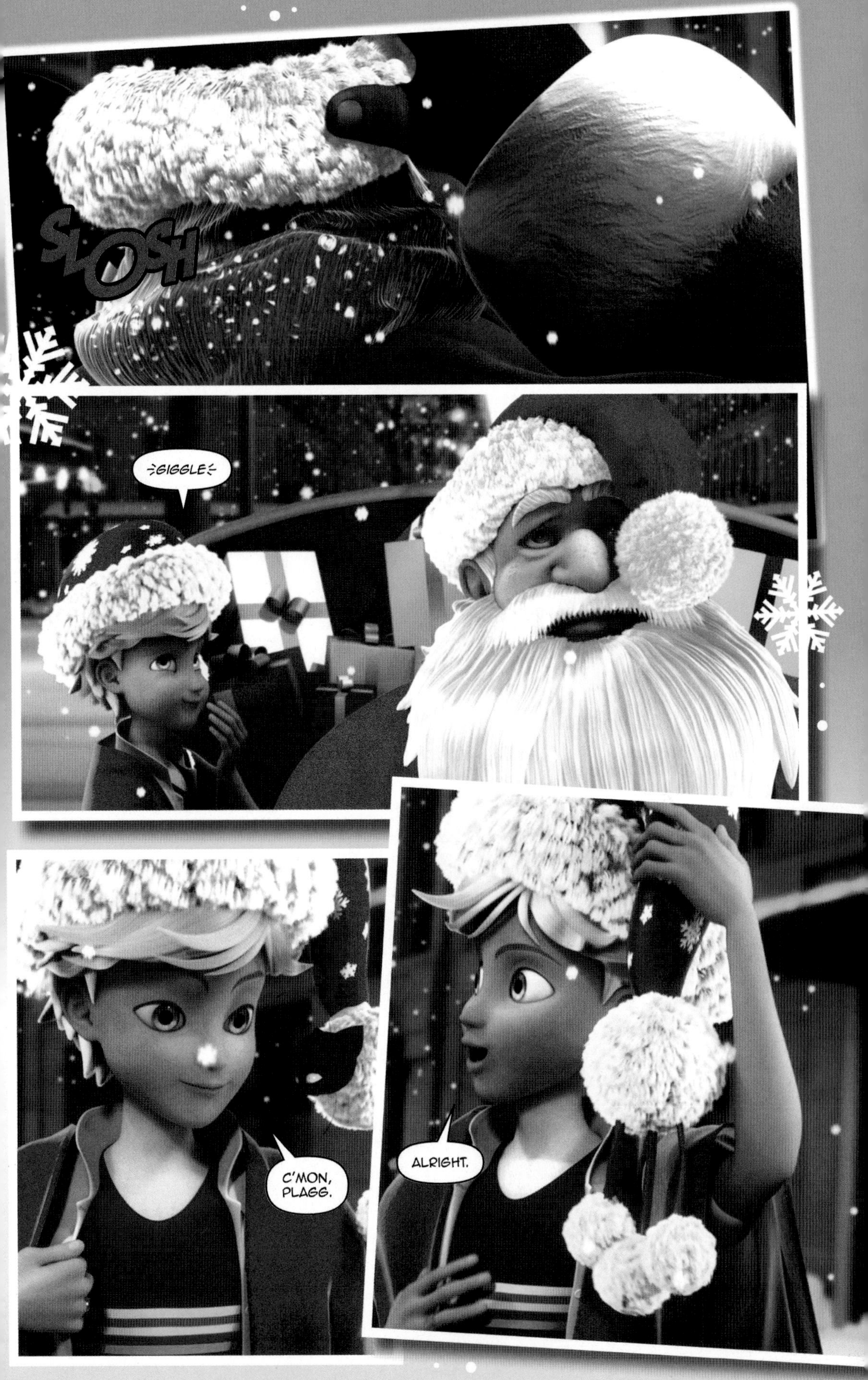
SLOSH
GIGGLE
C'MON, PLAGG.
ALRIGHT.

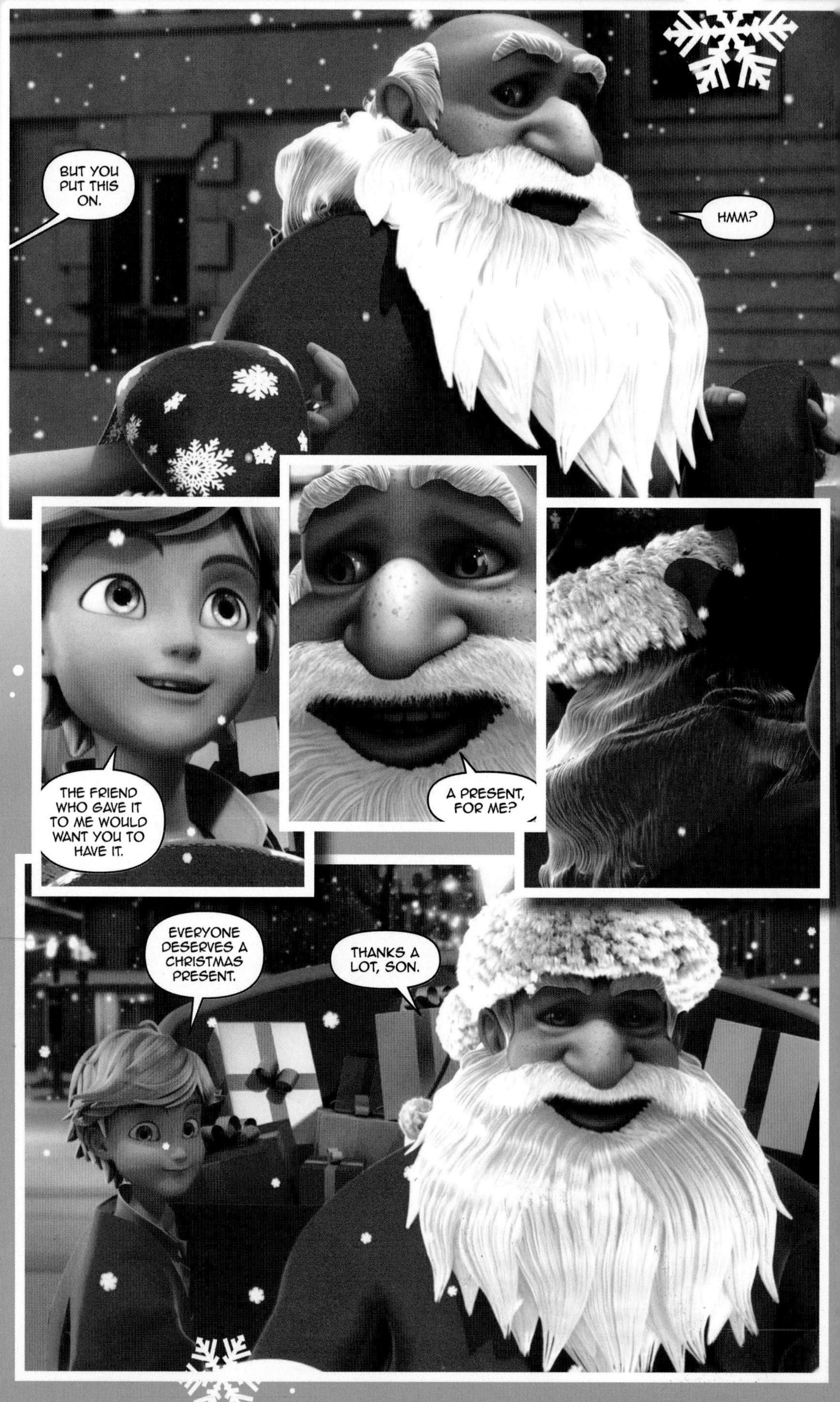
BUT YOU PUT THIS ON.
HMM?
THE FRIEND WHO GAVE IT TO ME WOULD WANT YOU TO HAVE IT.
A PRESENT, FOR ME?
EVERYONE DESERVES A CHRISTMAS PRESENT.
THANKS A LOT, SON.

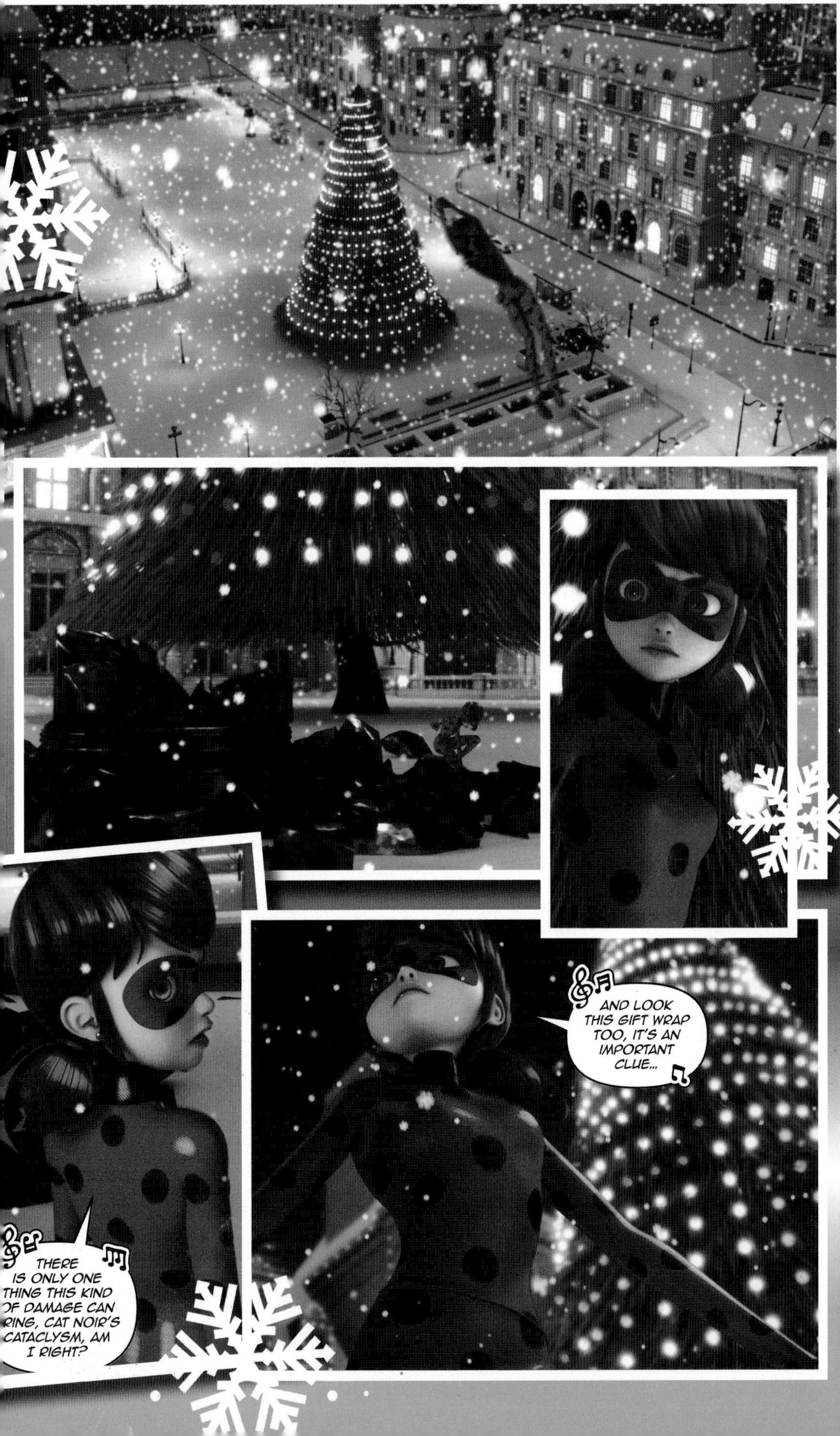
AND LOOK THIS GIFT WRAP TOO, IT'S AN IMPORTANT CLUE...
THERE IS ONLY ONE THING THIS KIND OF DAMAGE CAN BRING, CAT NOIR'S CATACLYSM, AM I RIGHT?

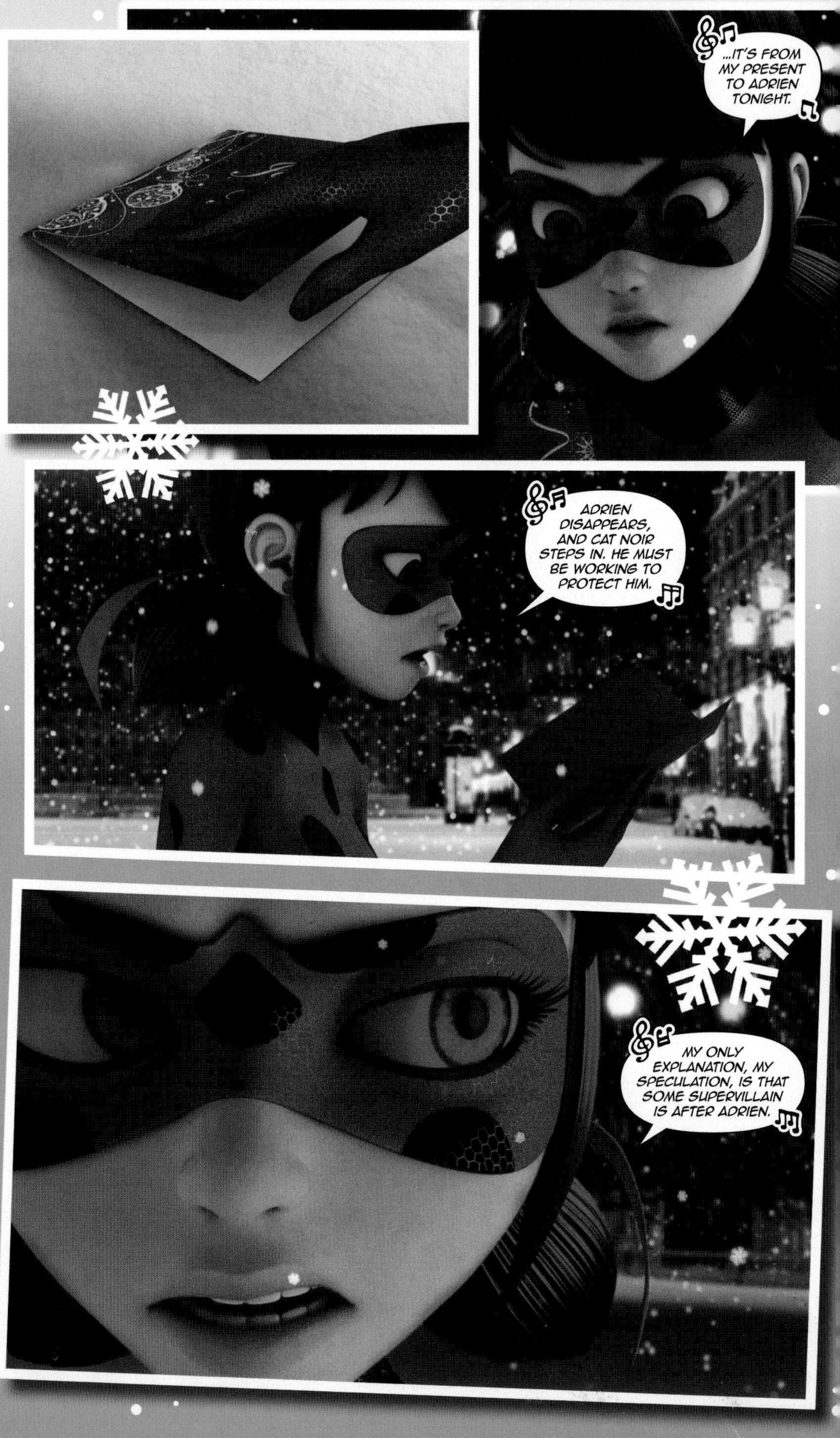
...IT'S FROM MY PRESENT TO ADRIEN TONIGHT.
ADRIEN DISAPPEARS, AND CAT NOIR STEPS IN. HE MUST BE WORKING TO PROTECT HIM.
MY ONLY EXPLANATION, MY SPECULATION, IS THAT SOME SUPERVILLAIN IS AFTER ADRIEN.

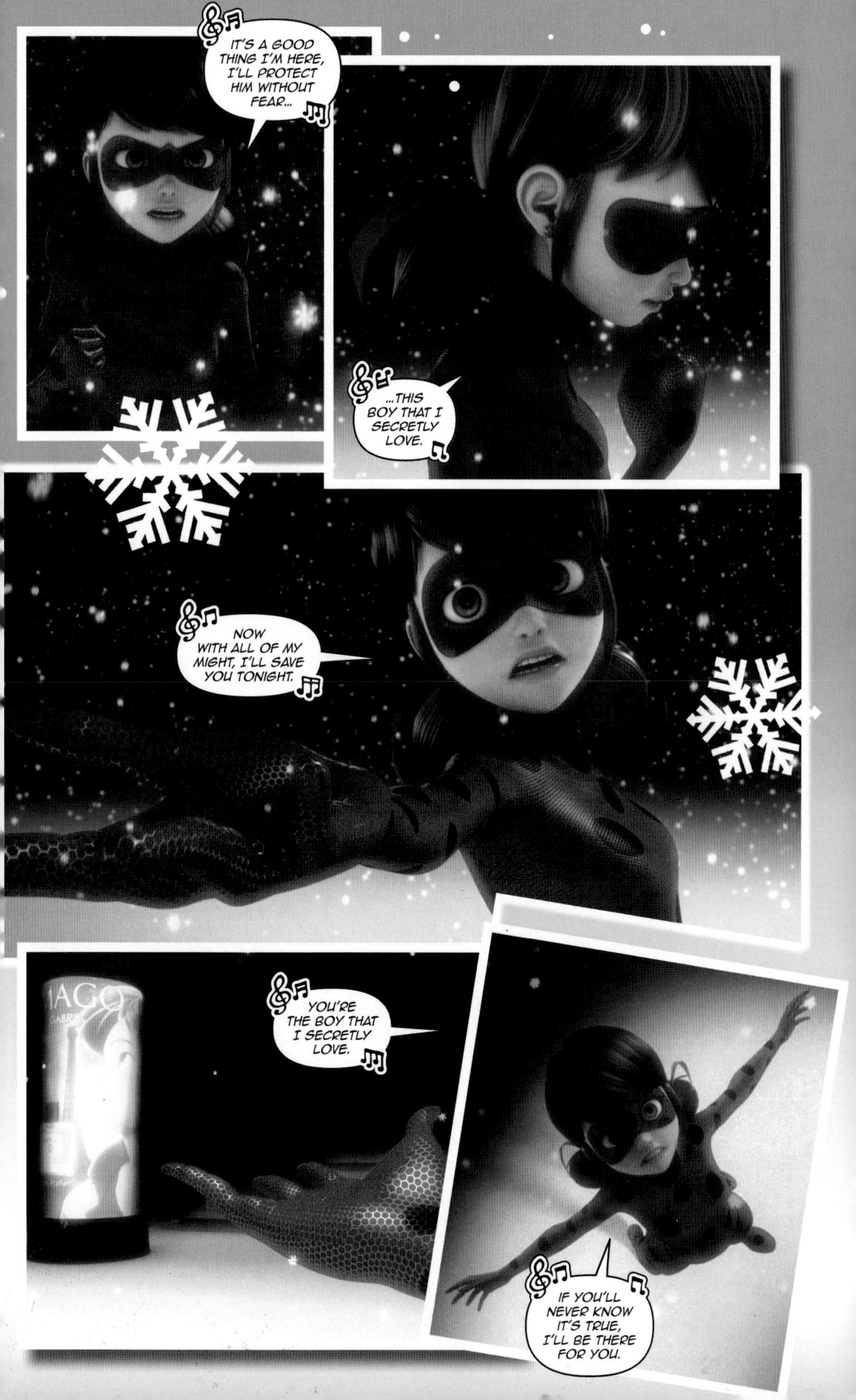
IT'S A GOOD THING I'M HERE, I'LL PROTECT HIM WITHOUT FEAR...
...THIS BOY THAT I SECRETLY LOVE.
NOW WITH ALL OF MY MIGHT, I'LL SAVE YOU TONIGHT.
YOU'RE THE BOY THAT I SECRETLY LOVE.
IF YOU'LL NEVER KNOW IT'S TRUE, I'LL BE THERE FOR YOU.

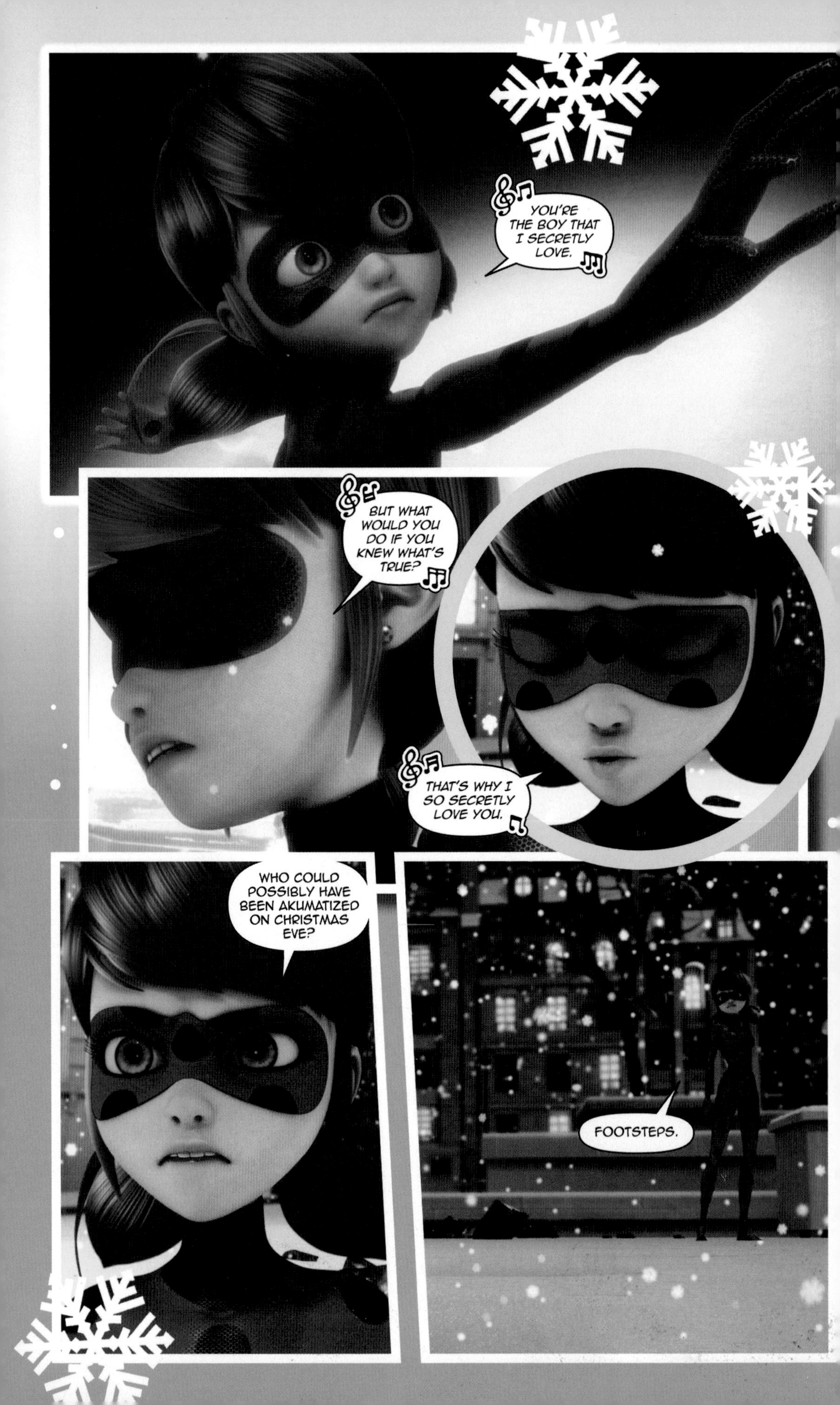
YOU'RE THE BOY THAT I SECRETLY LOVE.
BUT WHAT WOULD YOU DO IF YOU KNEW WHAT'S TRUE?
THAT'S WHY I SO SECRETLY LOVE YOU.
WHO COULD POSSIBLY HAVE BEEN AKUMATIZED ON CHRISTMAS EVE?
FOOTSTEPS.

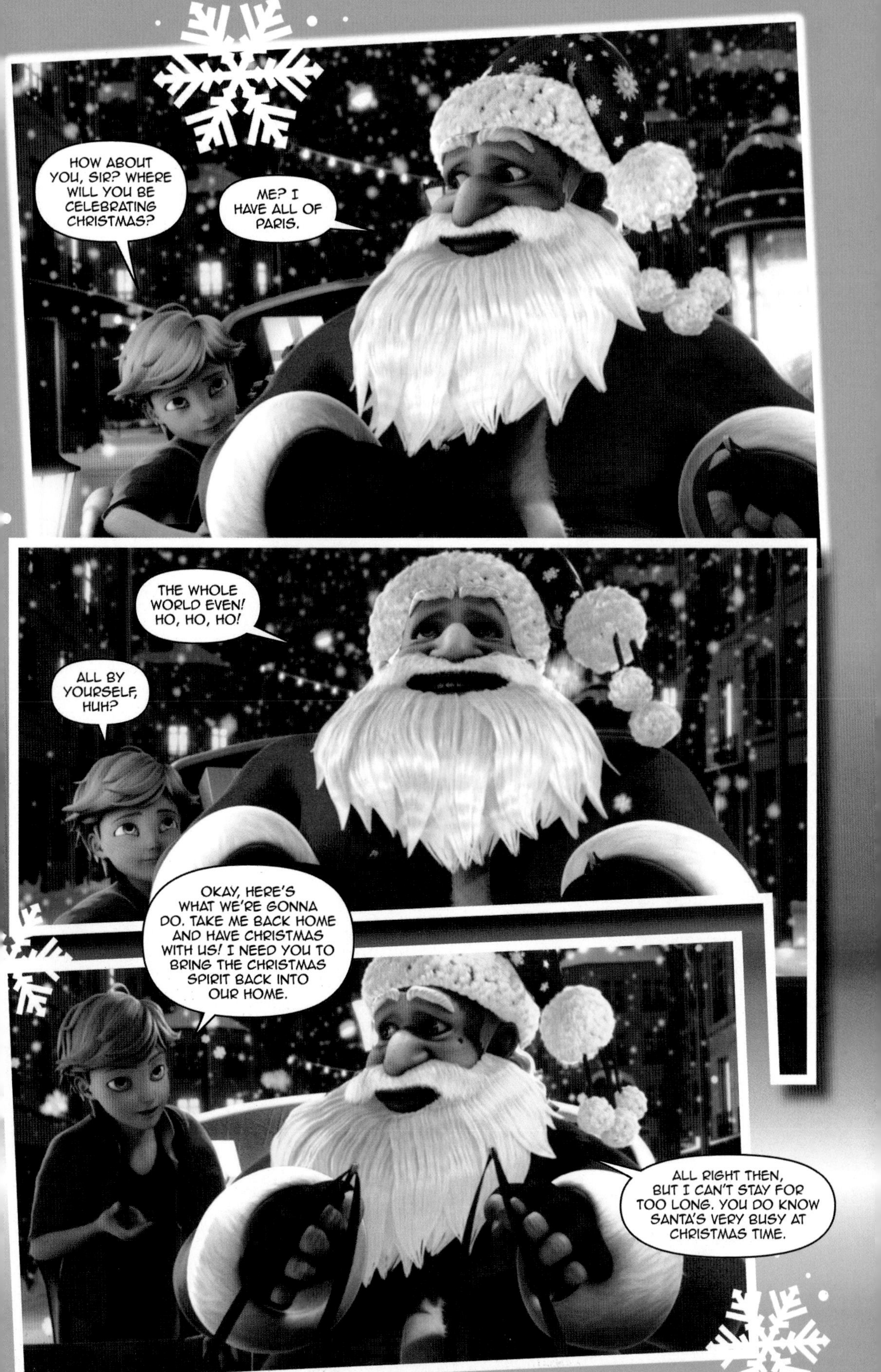
HOW ABOUT YOU, SIR? WHERE WILL YOU BE CELEBRATING CHRISTMAS?
ME? I HAVE ALL OF PARIS.
THE WHOLE WORLD EVEN! HO, HO, HO!
ALL BY YOURSELF, HUH?
OKAY, HERE'S WHAT WE'RE GONNA DO. TAKE ME BACK HOME AND HAVE CHRISTMAS WITH US! I NEED YOU TO BRING THE CHRISTMAS SPIRIT BACK INTO OUR HOME.
ALL RIGHT THEN, BUT I CAN'T STAY FOR TOO LONG. YOU DO KNOW SANTA'S VERY BUSY AT CHRISTMAS TIME.

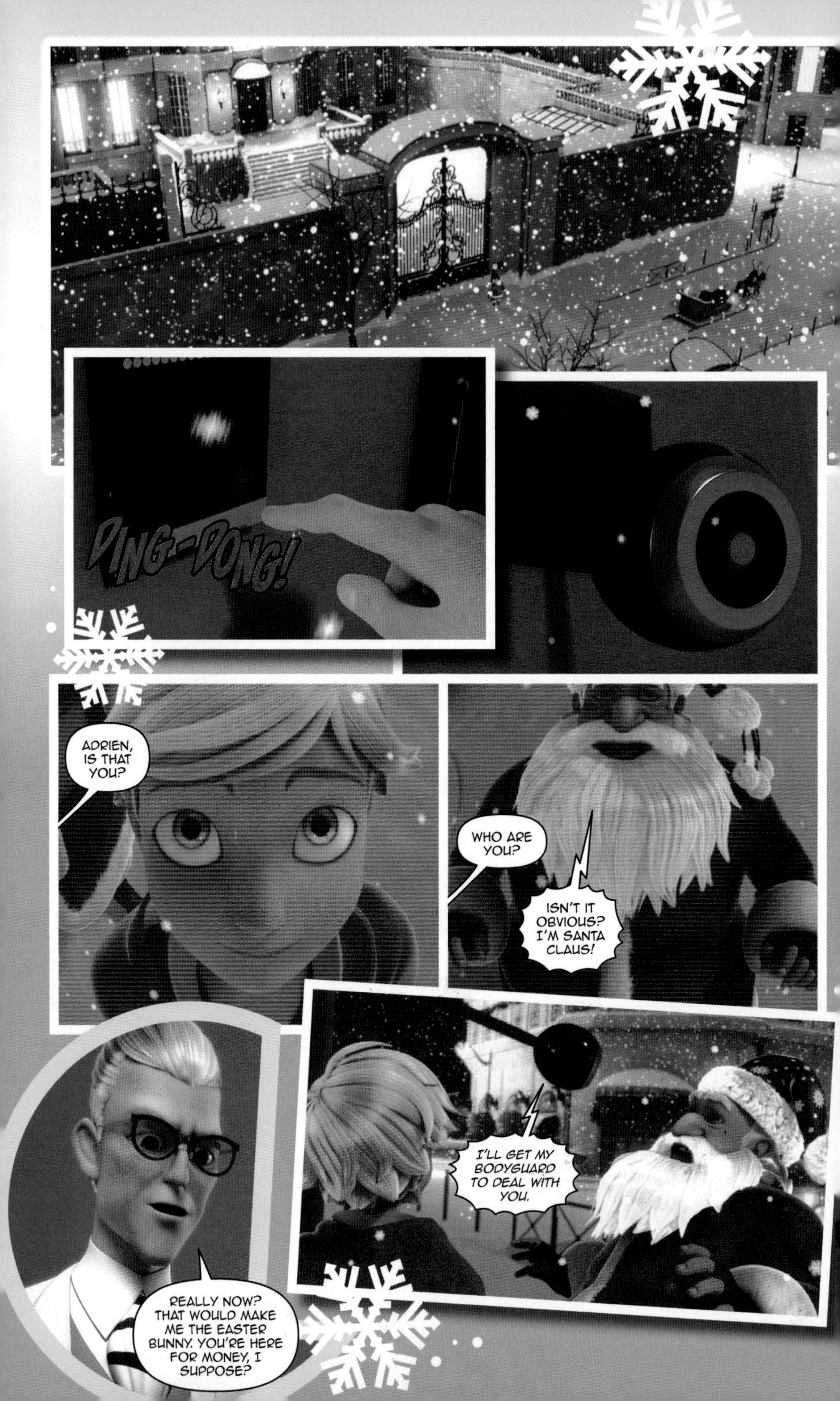
DING-DONG!
ADRIEN, IS THAT YOU?
WHO ARE YOU?
ISN'T IT OBVIOUS? I'M SANTA CLAUS!
REALLY NOW? THAT WOULD MAKE ME THE EASTER BUNNY. YOU'RE HERE FOR MONEY, I SUPPOSE?
I'LL GET MY BODYGUARD TO DEAL WITH YOU.

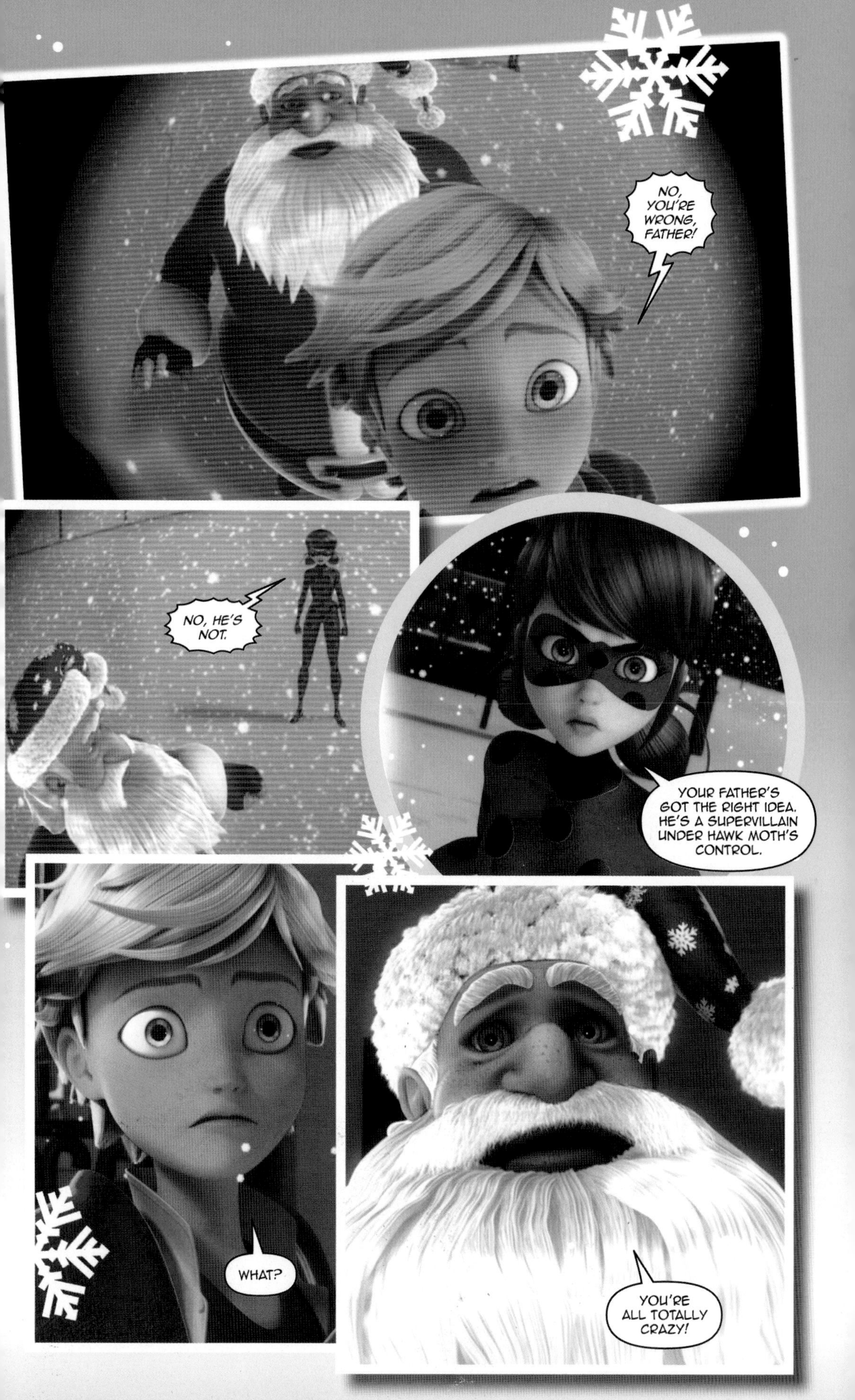
NO, YOU'RE WRONG, FATHER!
NO, HE'S NOT.
YOUR FATHER'S GOT THE RIGHT IDEA. HE'S A SUPERVILLAIN UNDER HAWK MOTH'S CONTROL.
WHAT?
YOU'RE ALL TOTALLY CRAZY!

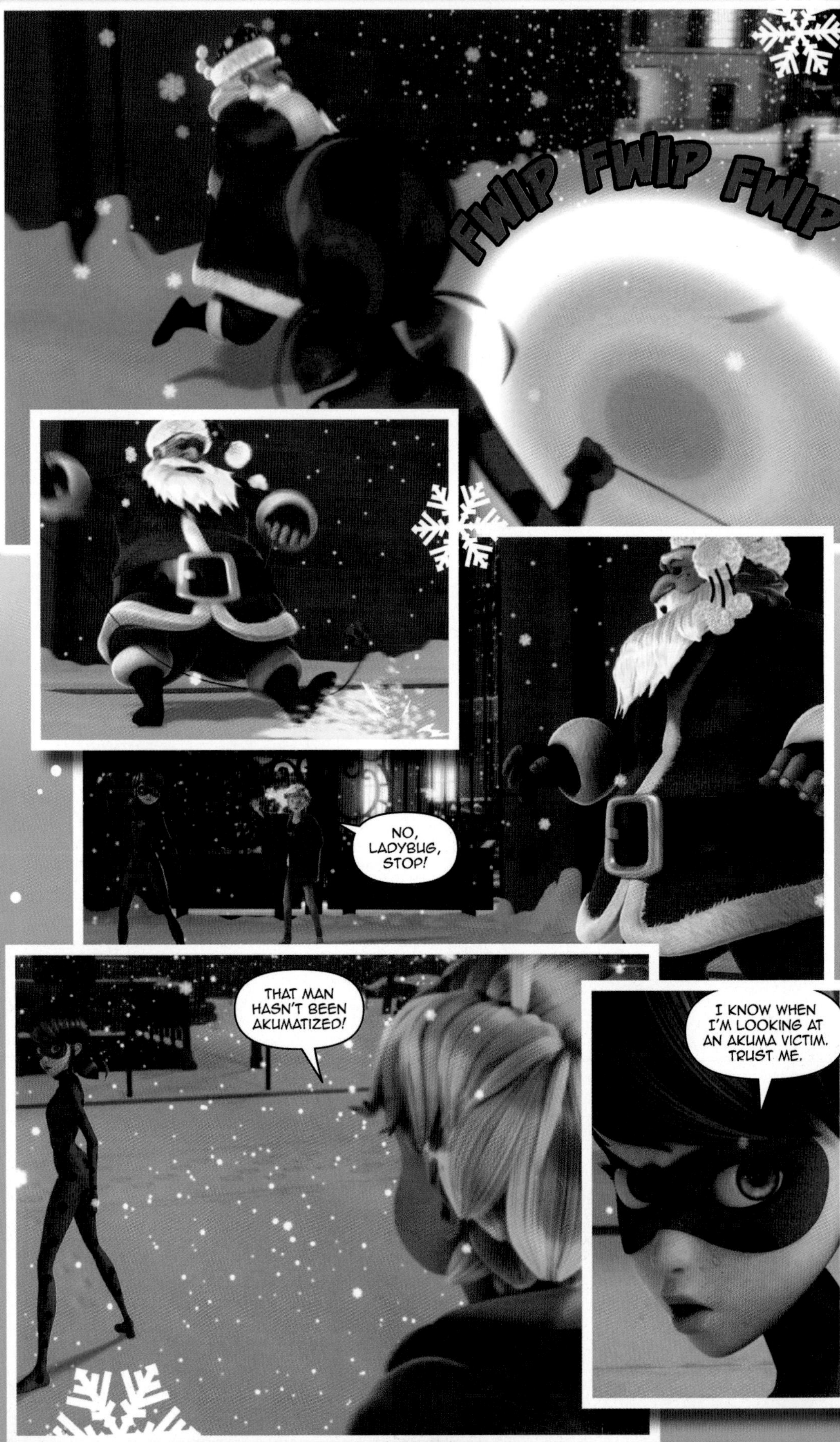
FWIP FWIP FWIP
NO, LADYBUG, STOP!
THAT MAN HASN'T BEEN AKUMATIZED!
I KNOW WHEN I'M LOOKING AT AN AKUMA VICTIM. TRUST ME.

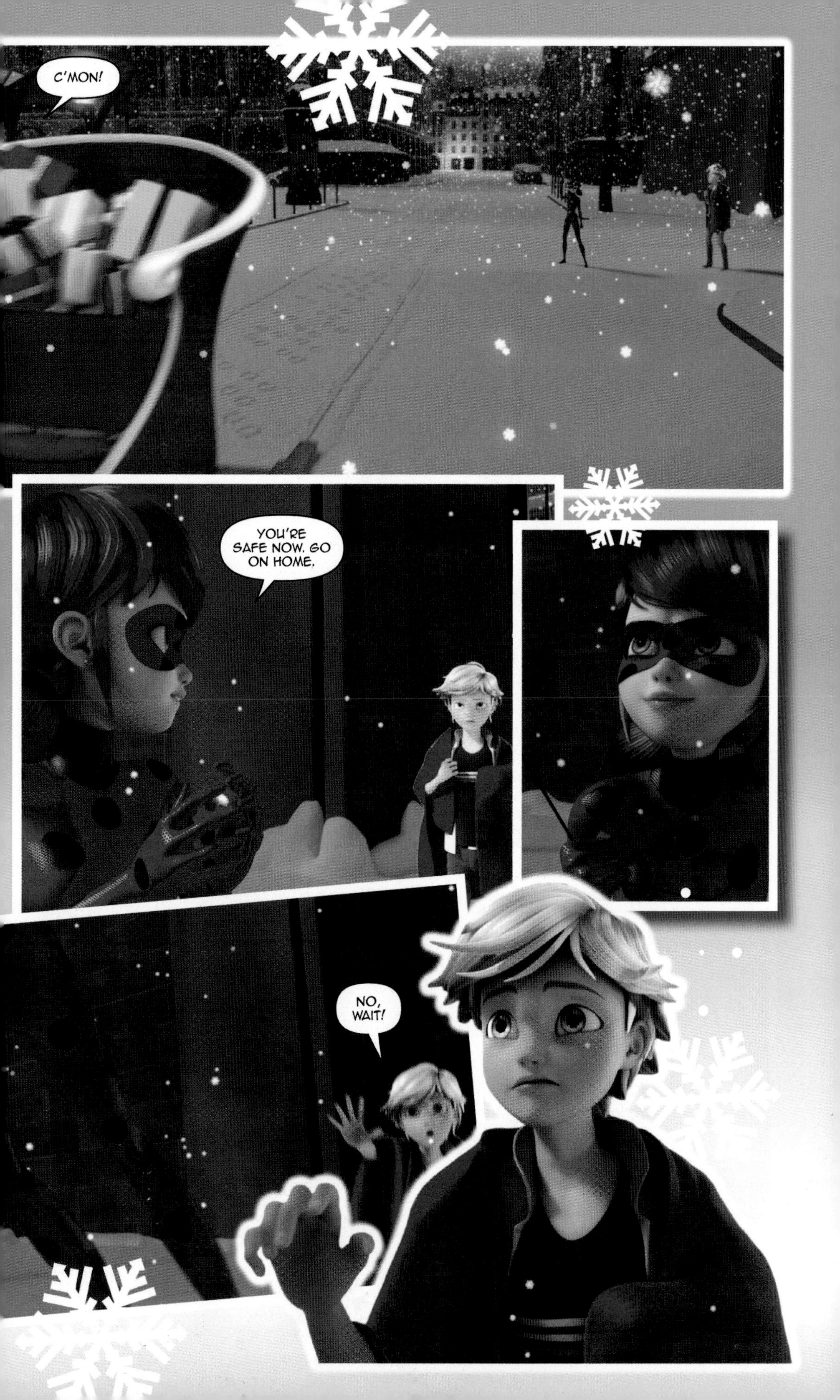
C'MON!
YOU'RE SAFE NOW. GO ON HOME.
NO, WAIT!

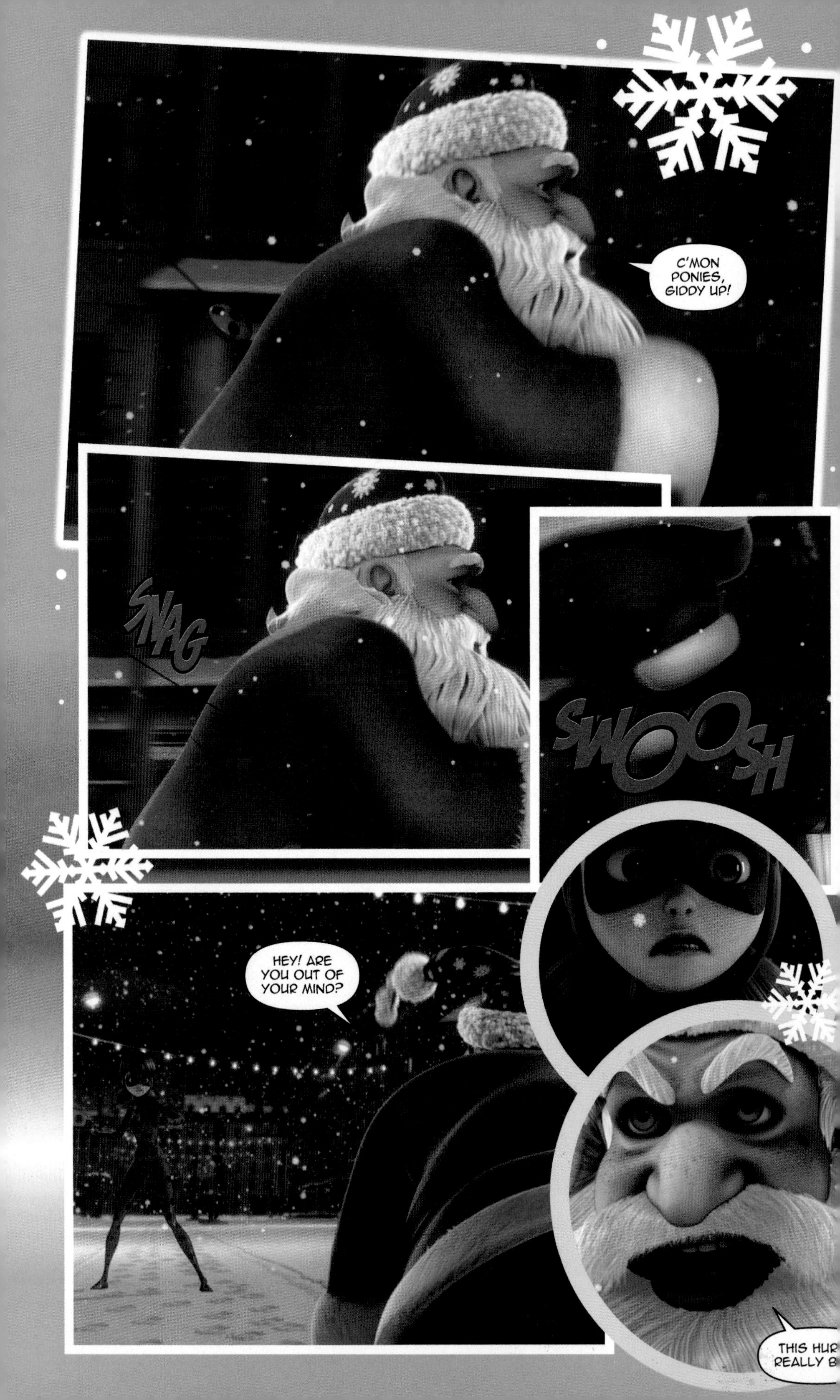
C'MON PONIES, GIDDY UP!
SNAG
SWOOSH
HEY! ARE YOU OUT OF YOUR MIND?
THIS HUR
REALLY B

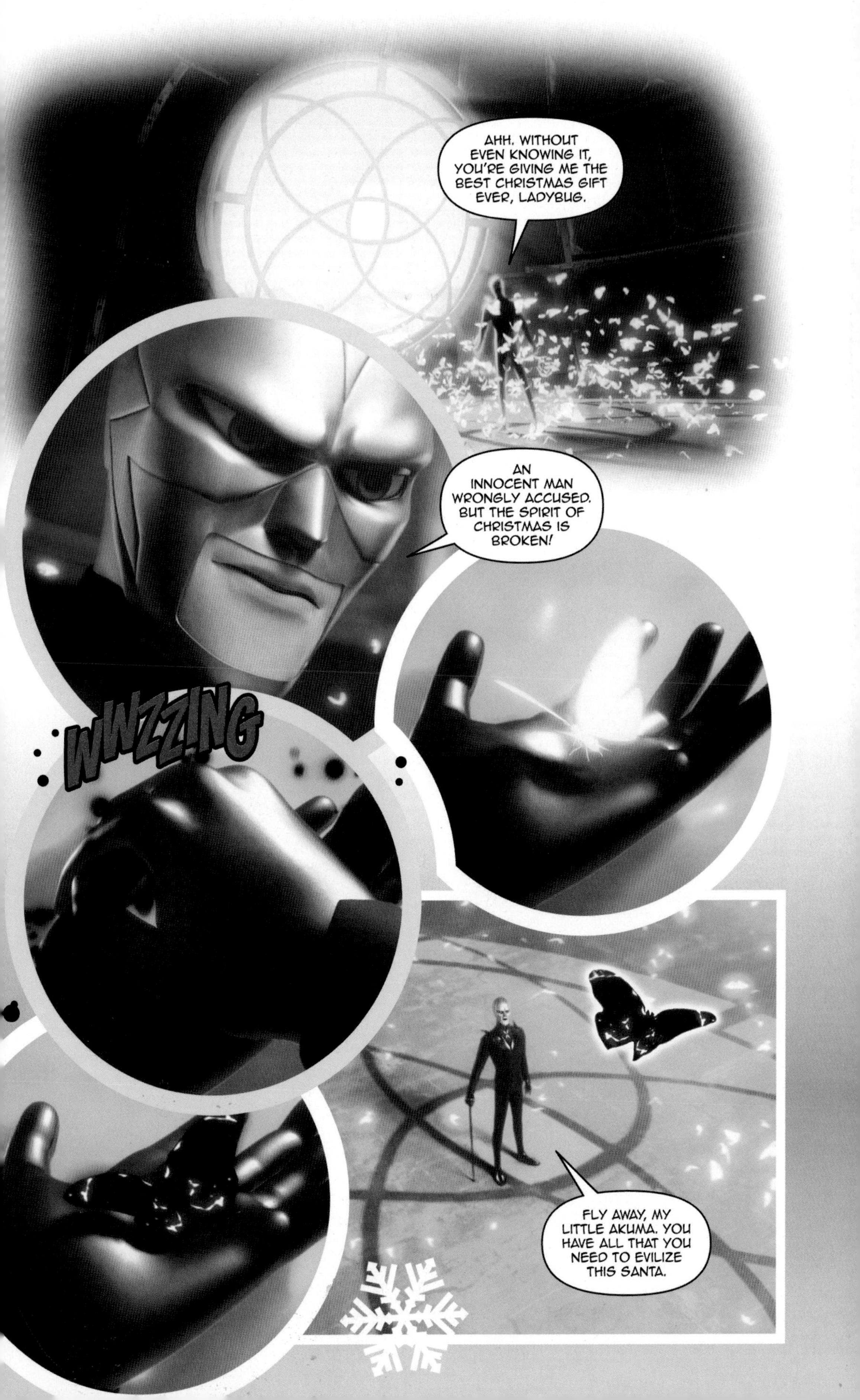
AHH. WITHOUT EVEN KNOWING IT, YOU'RE GIVING ME THE BEST CHRISTMAS GIFT EVER, LADYBUG.
AN INNOCENT MAN WRONGLY ACCUSED. BUT THE SPIRIT OF CHRISTMAS IS BROKEN!
WWZZING
FLY AWAY, MY LITTLE AKUMA. YOU HAVE ALL THAT YOU NEED TO EVILIZE THIS SANTA.

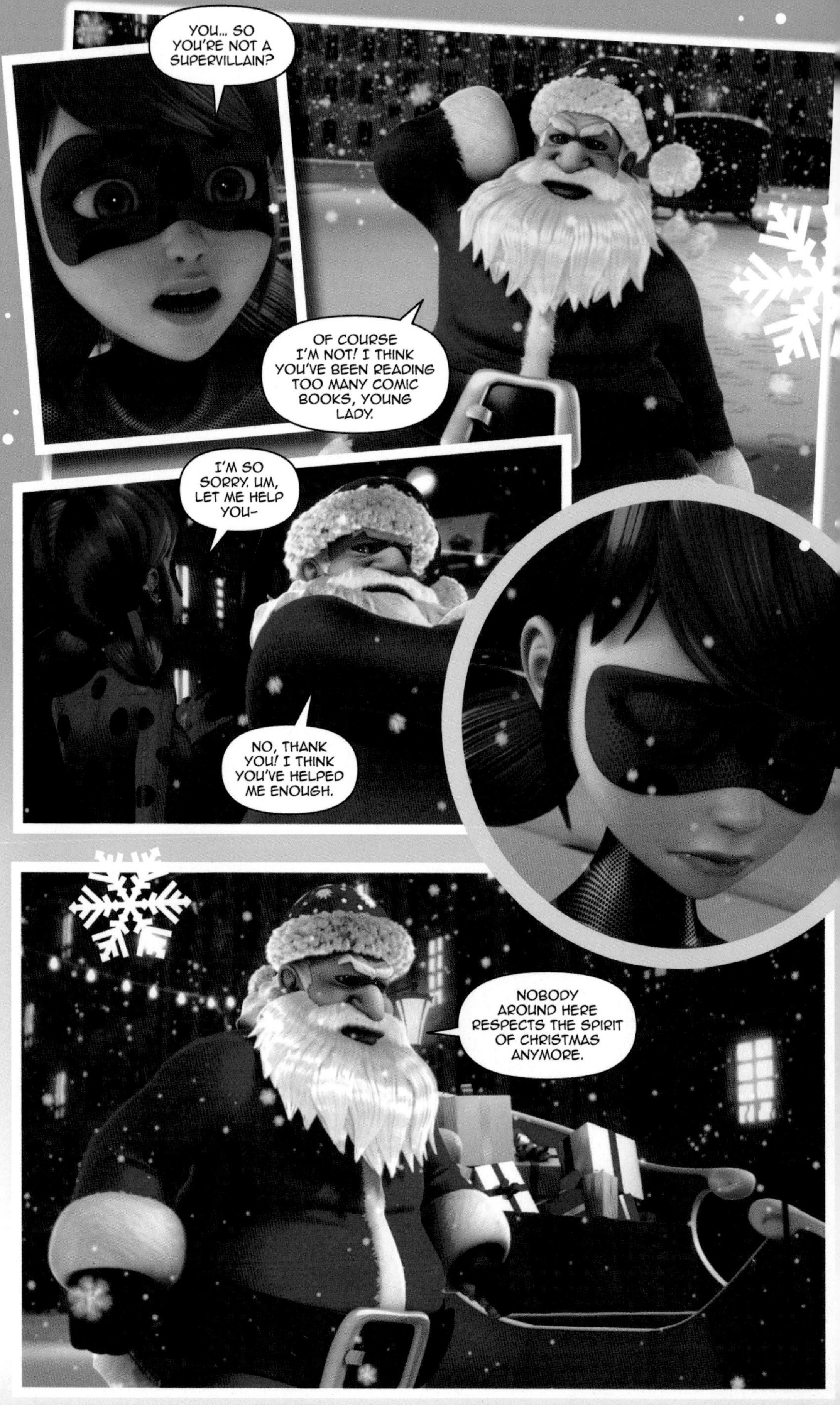
YOU... SO YOU'RE NOT A SUPERVILLAIN?
OF COURSE I'M NOT! I THINK YOU'VE BEEN READING TOO MANY COMIC BOOKS, YOUNG LADY.
I'M SO SORRY. UM, LET ME HELP YOU-
NO, THANK YOU! I THINK YOU'VE HELPED ME ENOUGH.
NOBODY AROUND HERE RESPECTS THE SPIRIT OF CHRISTMAS ANYMORE.

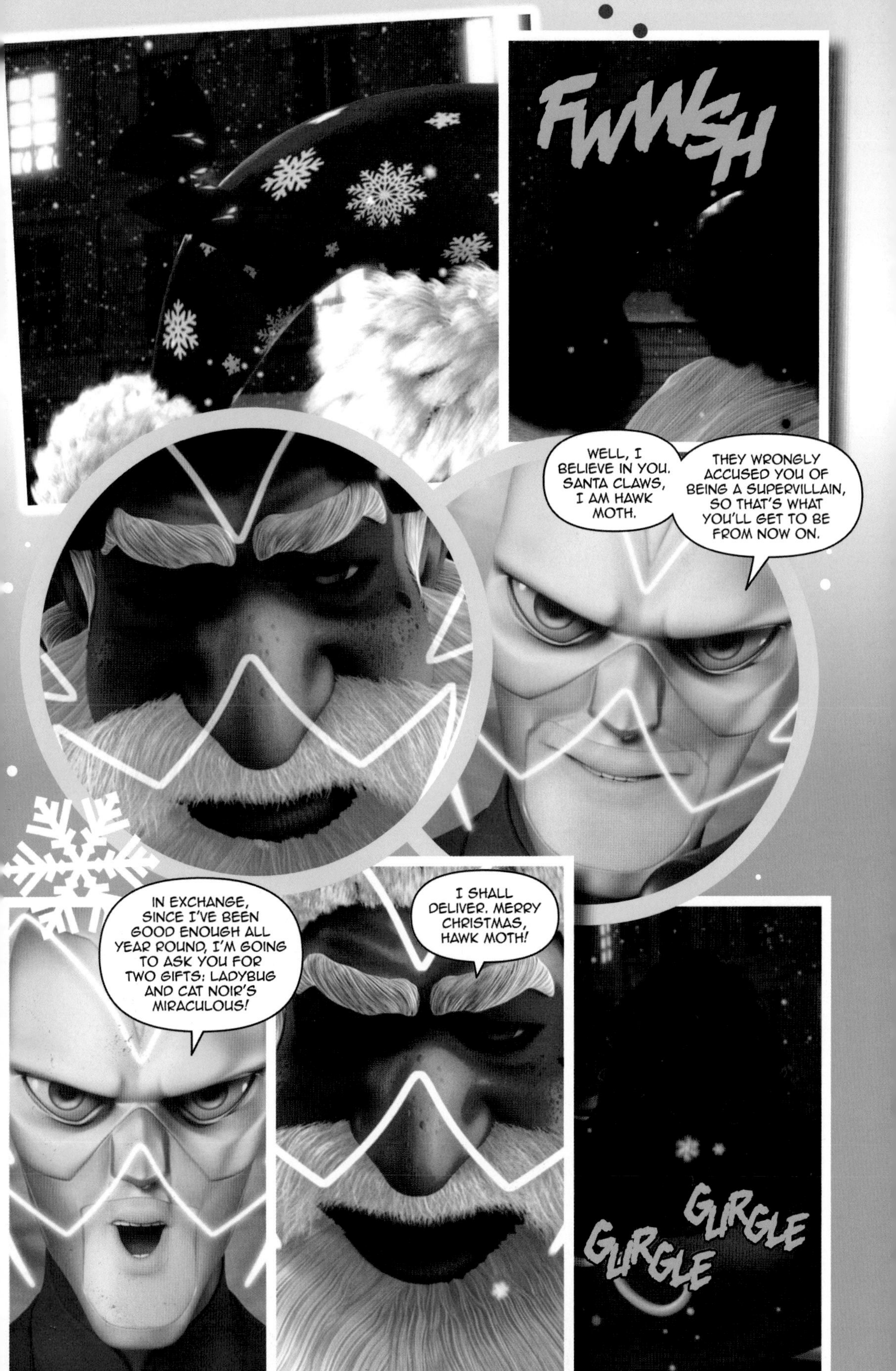
FWUSH
WELL, I BELIEVE IN YOU. SANTA CLAWS, I AM HAWK MOTH.
THEY WRONGLY ACCUSED YOU OF BEING A SUPERVILLAIN, SO THAT'S WHAT YOU'LL GET TO BE FROM NOW ON.
IN EXCHANGE, SINCE I'VE BEEN GOOD ENOUGH ALL YEAR ROUND, I'M GOING TO ASK YOU FOR TWO GIFTS: LADYBUG AND CAT NOIR'S MIRACULOUS!
I SHALL DELIVER. MERRY CHRISTMAS, HAWK MOTH!
GURGLE
GURGLE

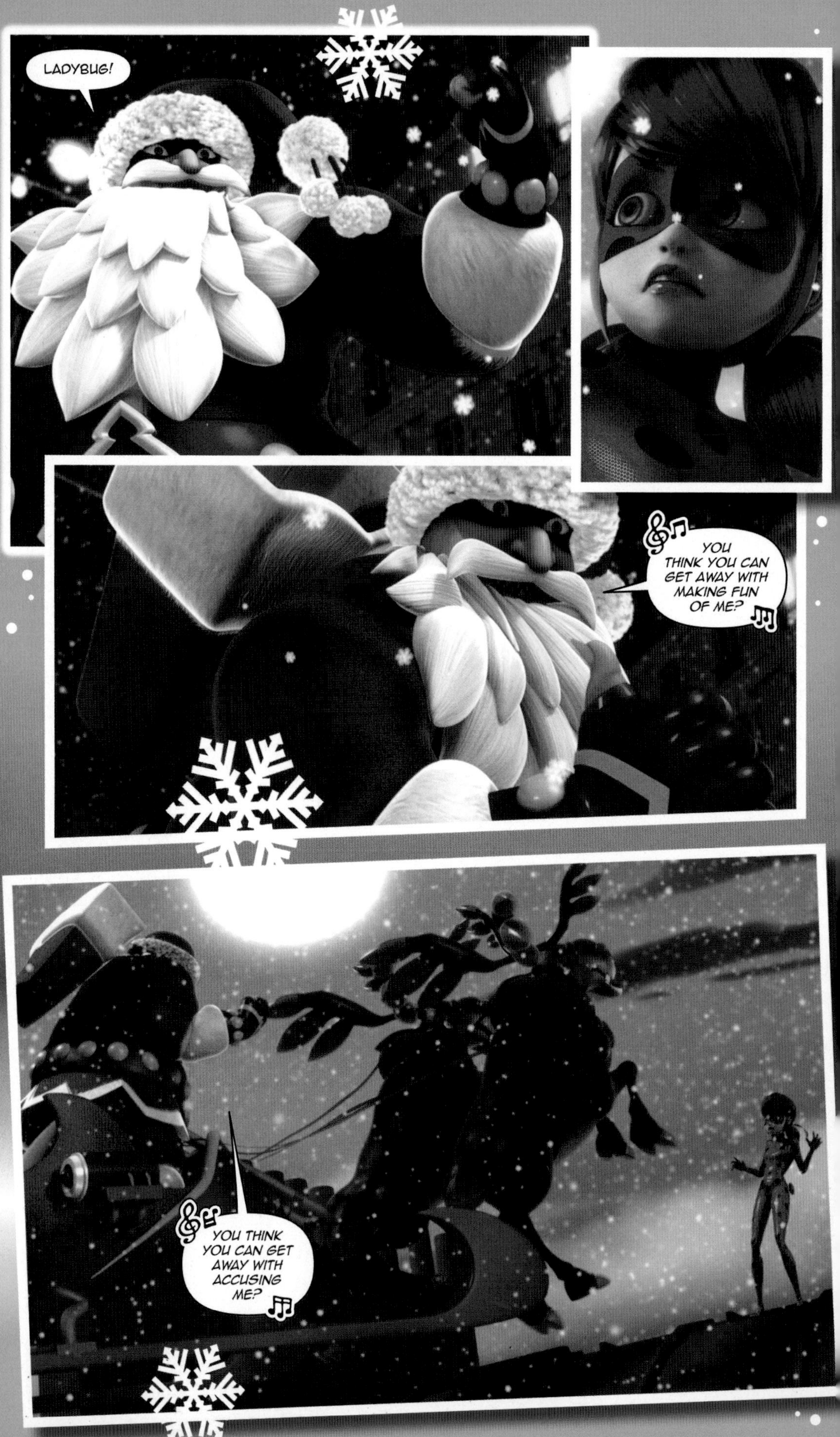

LADYBUG!
YOU THINK YOU CAN GET AWAY WITH MAKING FUN OF ME?
YOU THINK YOU CAN GET AWAY WITH ACCUSING ME?

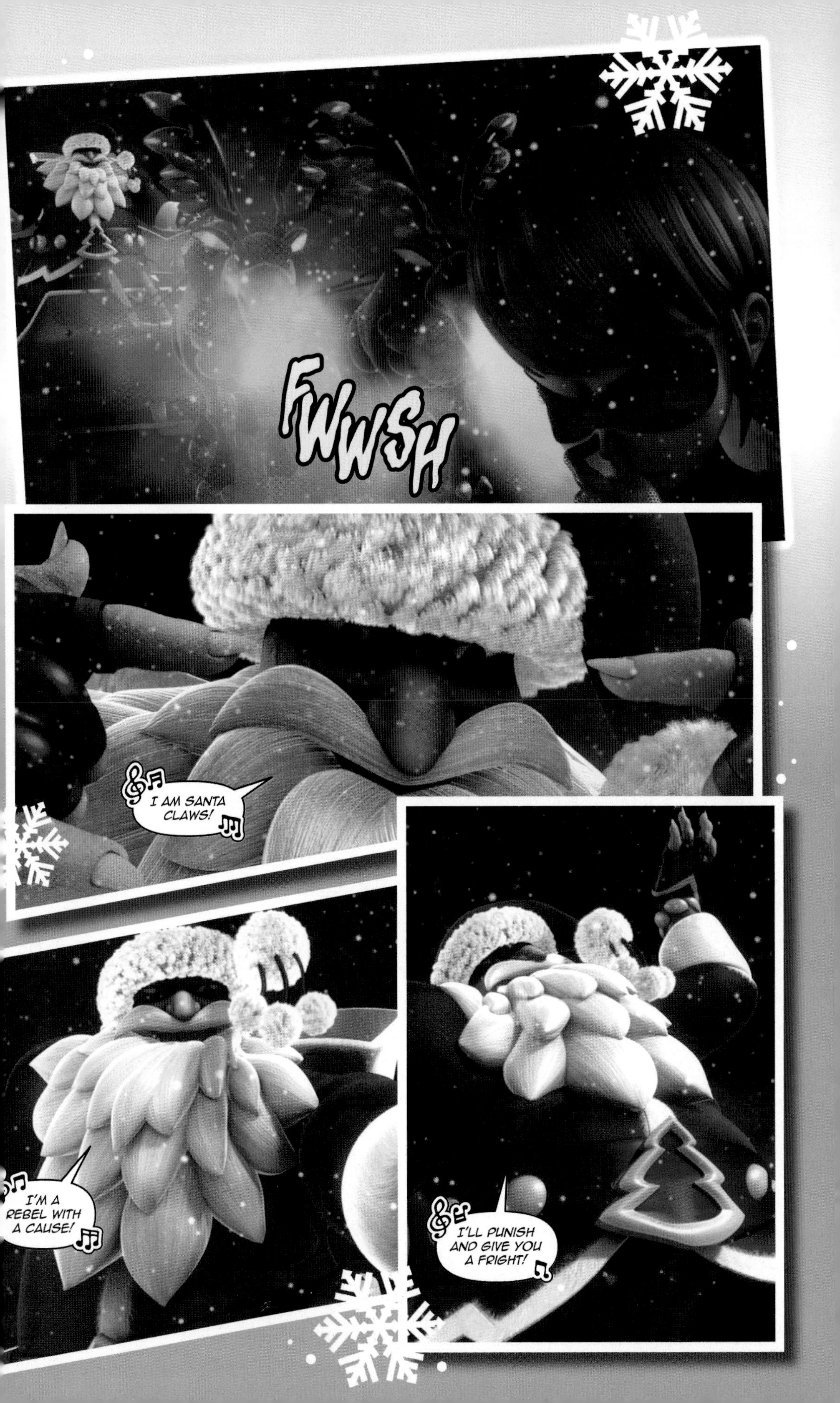

FWWSH
I AM SANTA CLAWS!
I'M A REBEL WITH A CAUSE!
I'LL PUNISH AND GIVE YOU A FRIGHT!

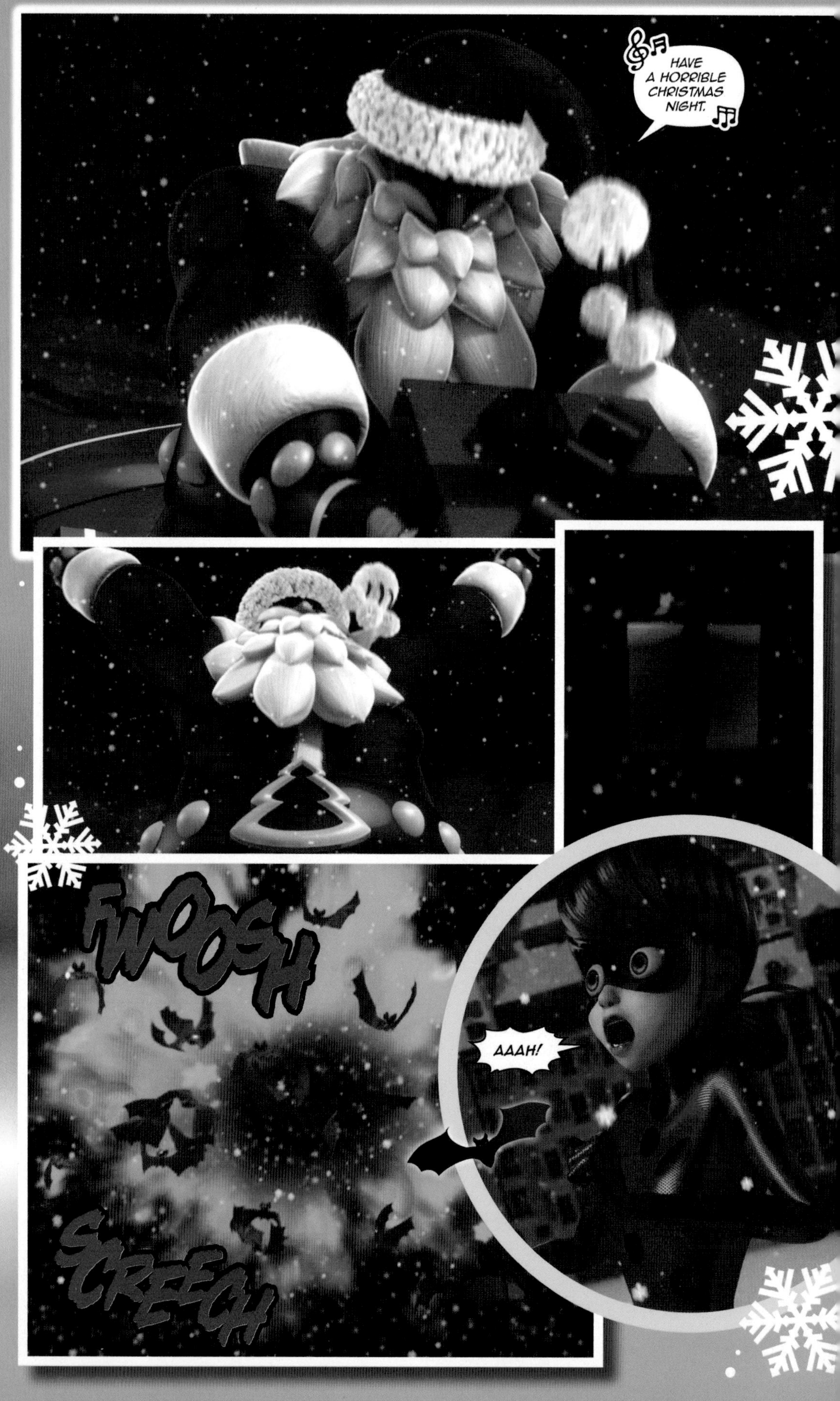
HAVE A HORRIBLE CHRISTMAS NIGHT.
FWOOSH
AAAH!
SCREECH

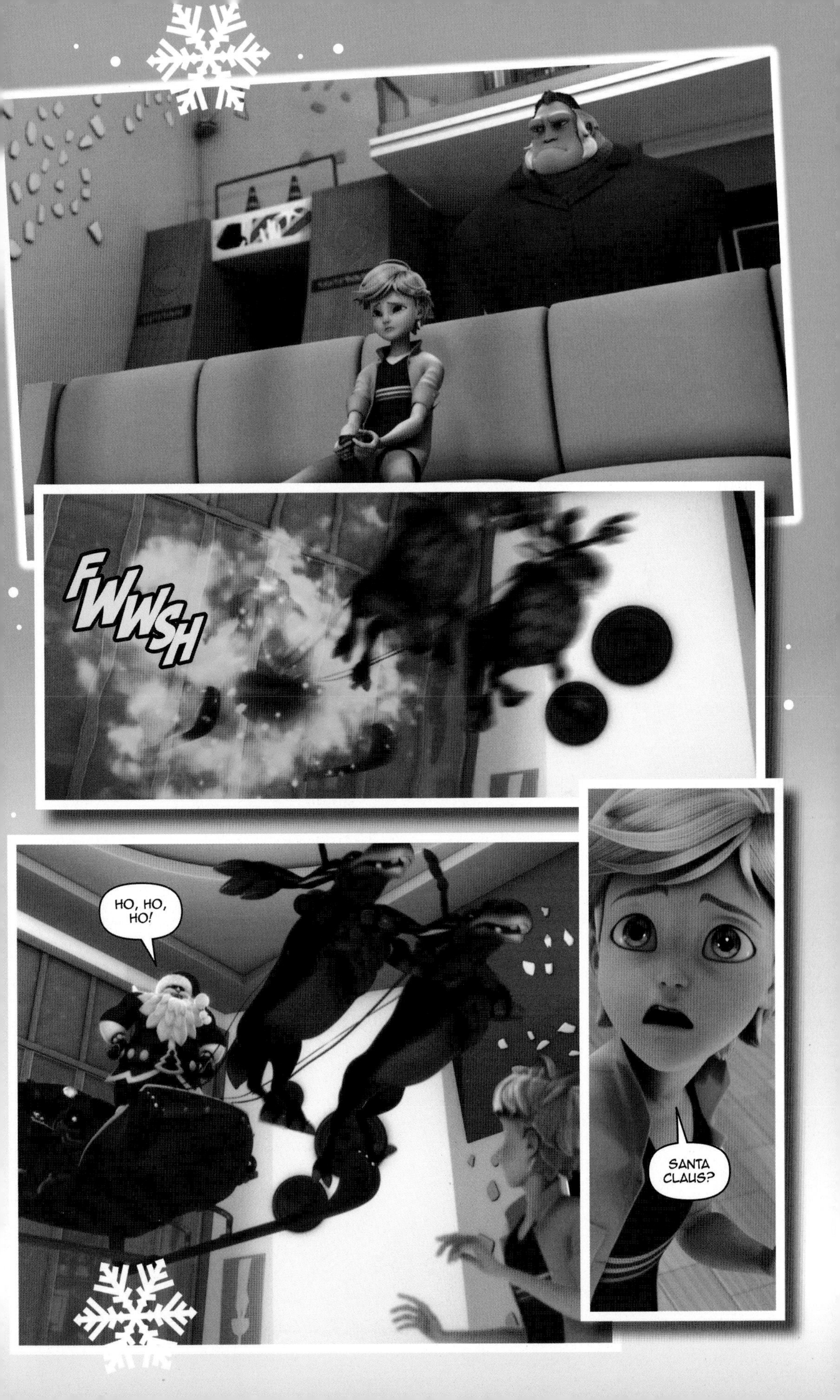

FWWSH
HO, HO, HO!
SANTA CLAUS?

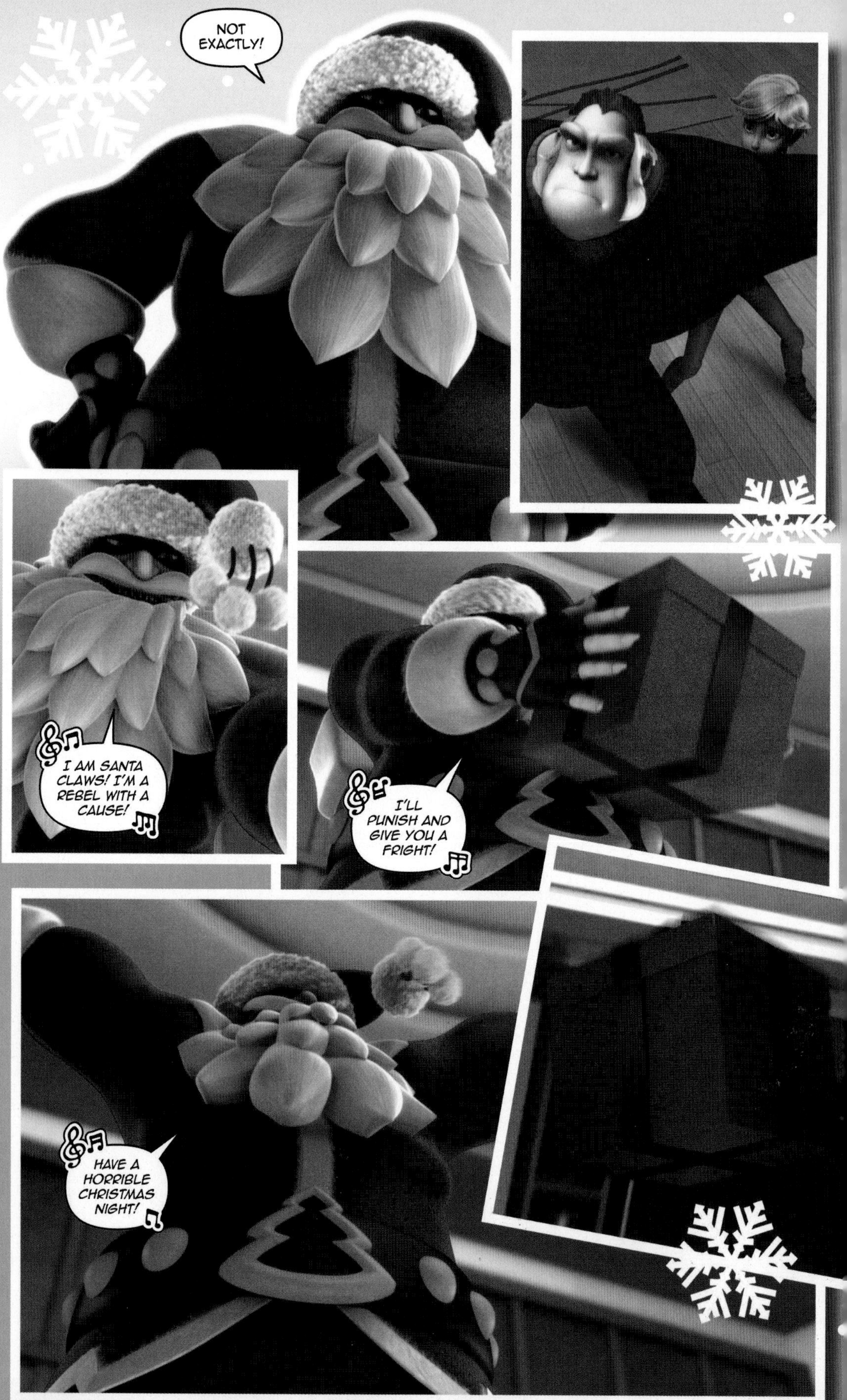
NOT EXACTLY!
I AM SANTA CLAWS! I'M A REBEL WITH A CAUSE!
I'LL PUNISH AND GIVE YOU A FRIGHT!
HAVE A HORRIBLE CHRISTMAS NIGHT!

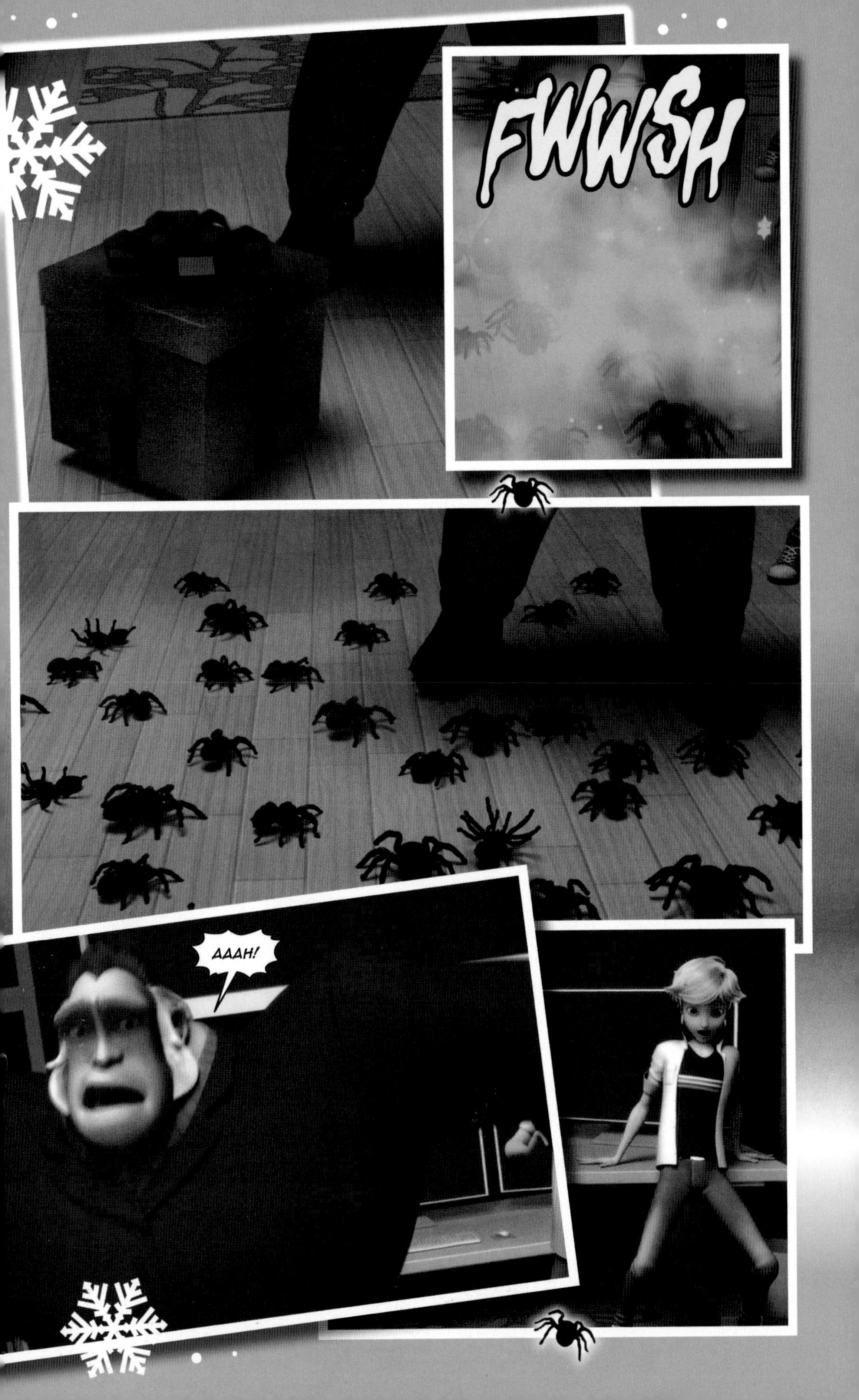
FWWSH
AAAH!

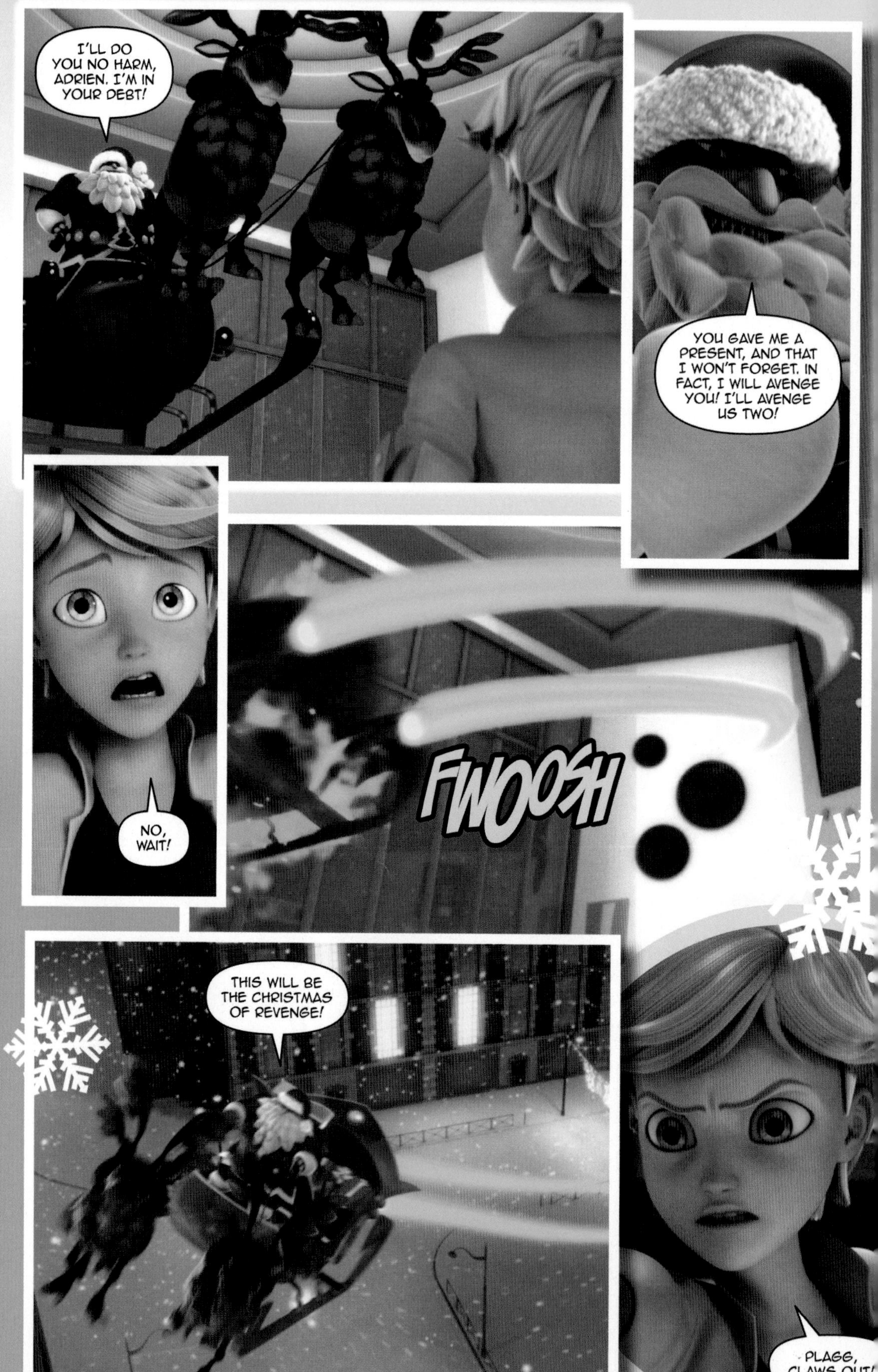
I'LL DO YOU NO HARM, ADRIEN. I'M IN YOUR DEBT!
YOU GAVE ME A PRESENT, AND THAT I WON'T FORGET. IN FACT, I WILL AVENGE YOU! I'LL AVENGE US TWO!
NO, WAIT!
FWOOSH
THIS WILL BE THE CHRISTMAS OF REVENGE!
PLAGG, CLAWS OUT!

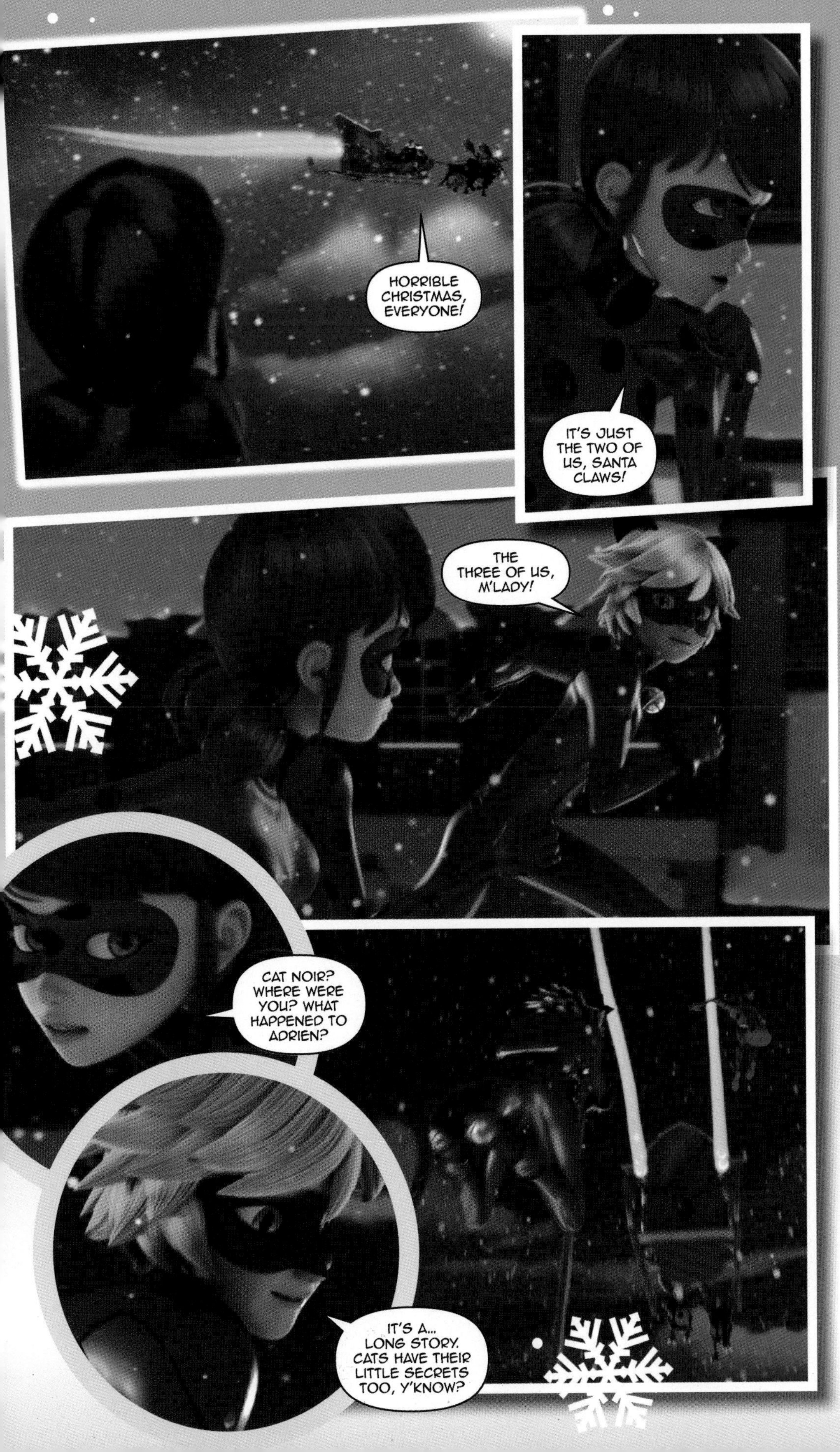
HORRIBLE CHRISTMAS, EVERYONE!
IT'S JUST THE TWO OF US, SANTA CLAWS!
THE THREE OF US, M'LADY!
CAT NOIR? WHERE WERE YOU? WHAT HAPPENED TO ADRIEN?
IT'S A... LONG STORY. CATS HAVE THEIR LITTLE SECRETS TOO, Y'KNOW?

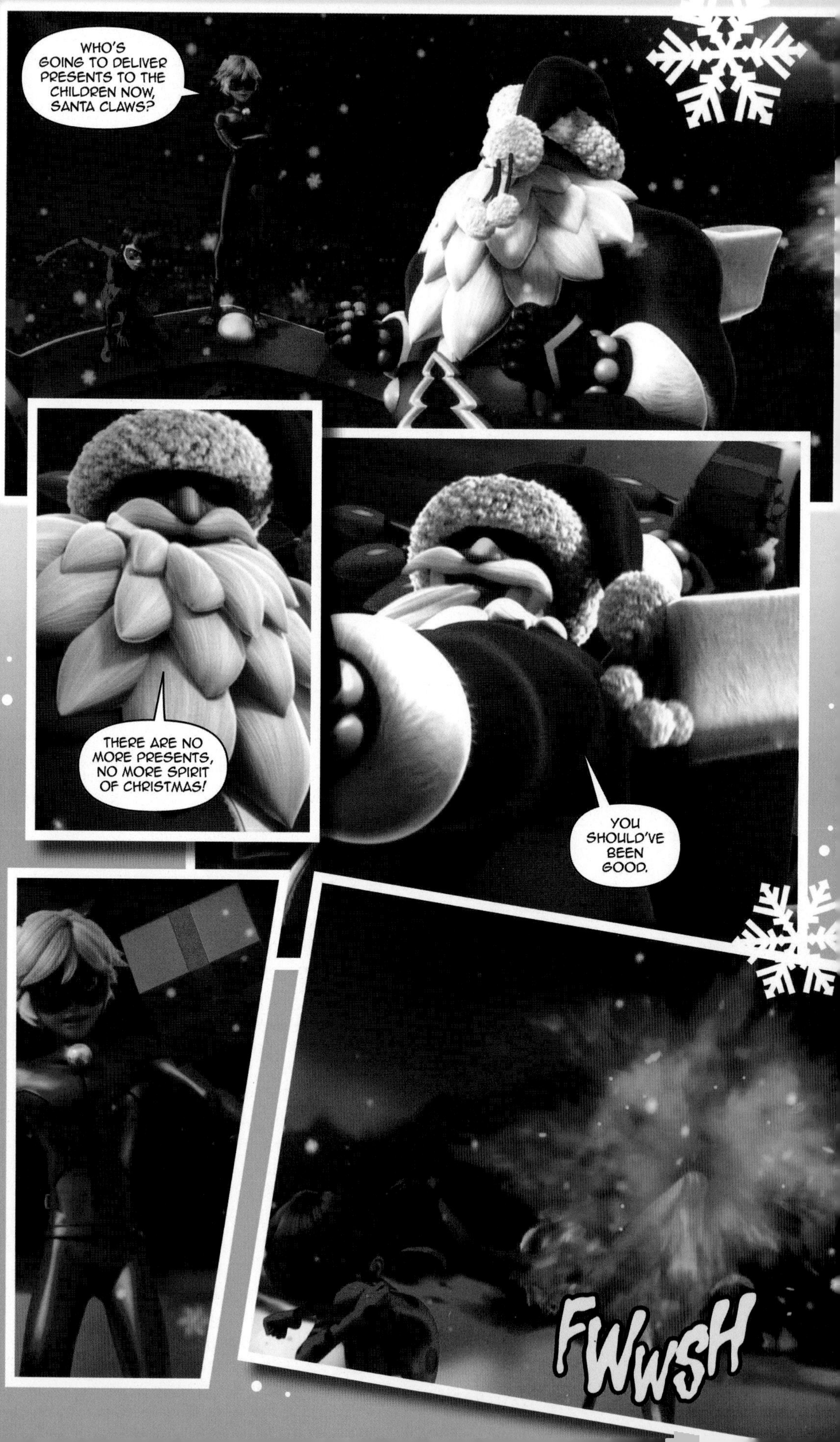

WHO'S GOING TO DELIVER PRESENTS TO THE CHILDREN NOW, SANTA CLAWS?
THERE ARE NO MORE PRESENTS, NO MORE SPIRIT OF CHRISTMAS!
YOU SHOULD'VE BEEN GOOD.
FWWSH

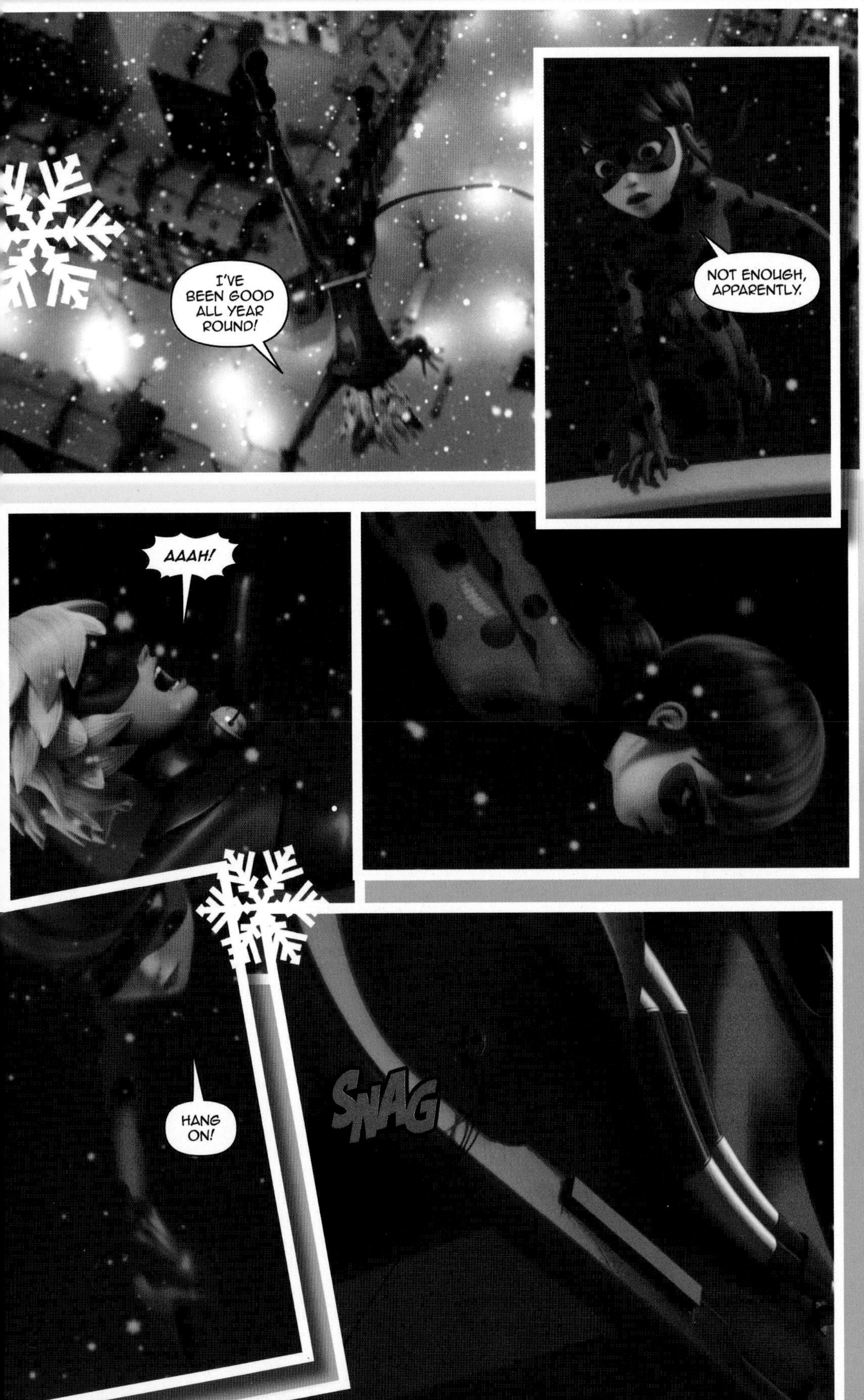
I'VE BEEN GOOD ALL YEAR ROUND!
NOT ENOUGH, APPARENTLY.
AAAH!
HANG ON!
SNAG

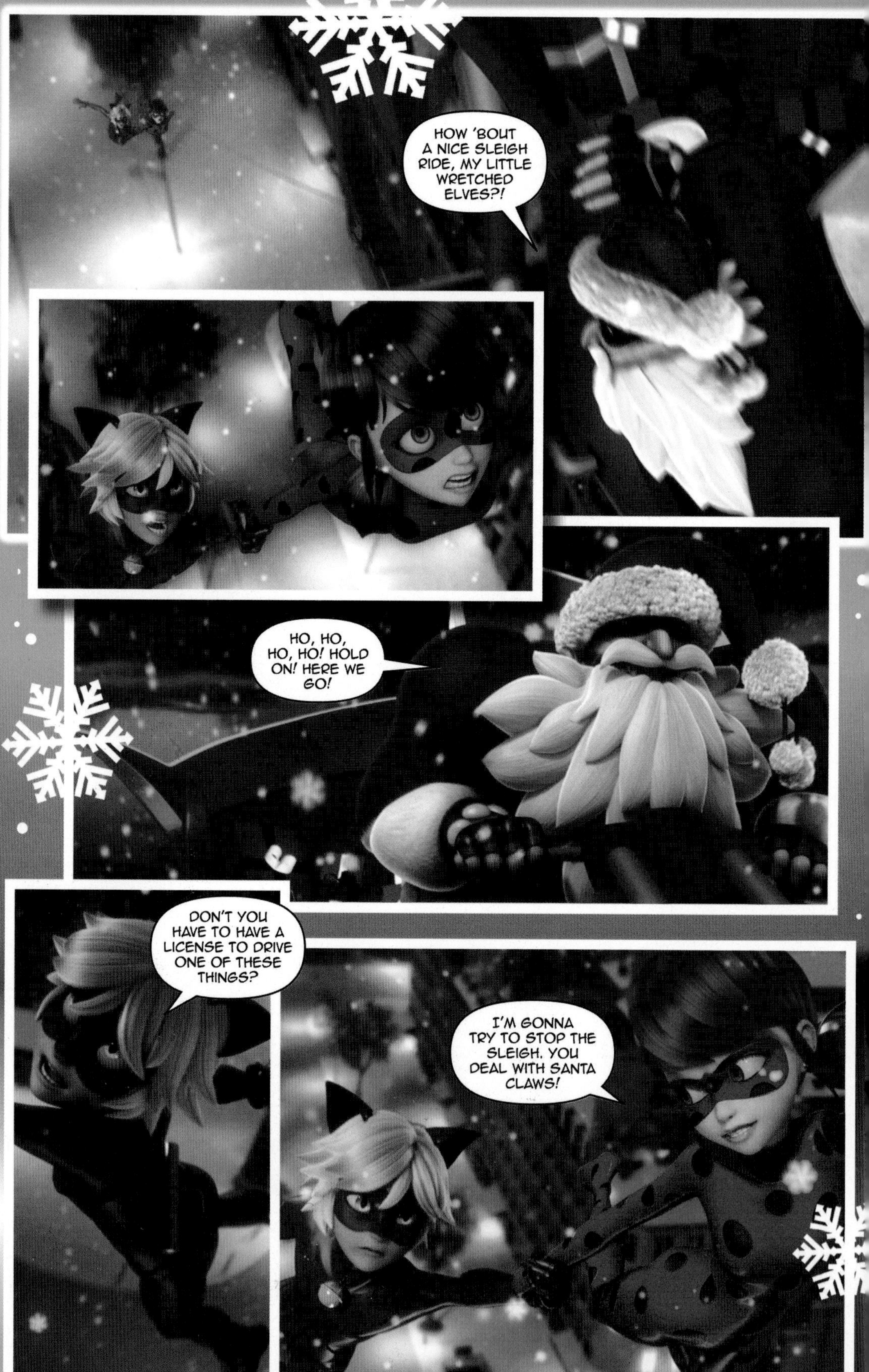
HOW 'BOUT A NICE SLEIGH RIDE, MY LITTLE WRETCHED ELVES?!
HO, HO, HO, HO! HOLD ON! HERE WE GO!
DON'T YOU HAVE TO HAVE A LICENSE TO DRIVE ONE OF THESE THINGS?
I'M GONNA TRY TO STOP THE SLEIGH. YOU DEAL WITH SANTA CLAWS!

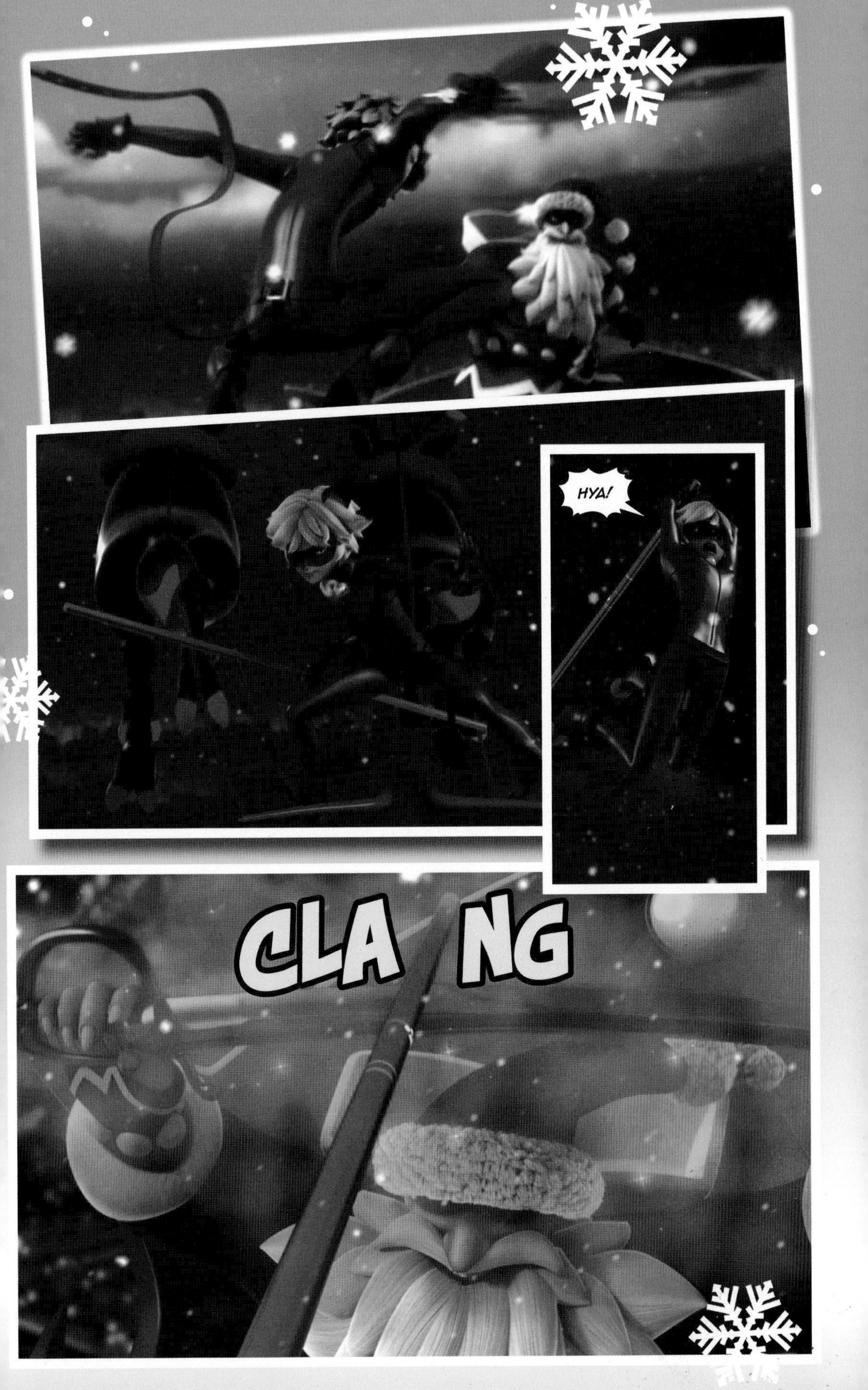
HYA!
CLANG

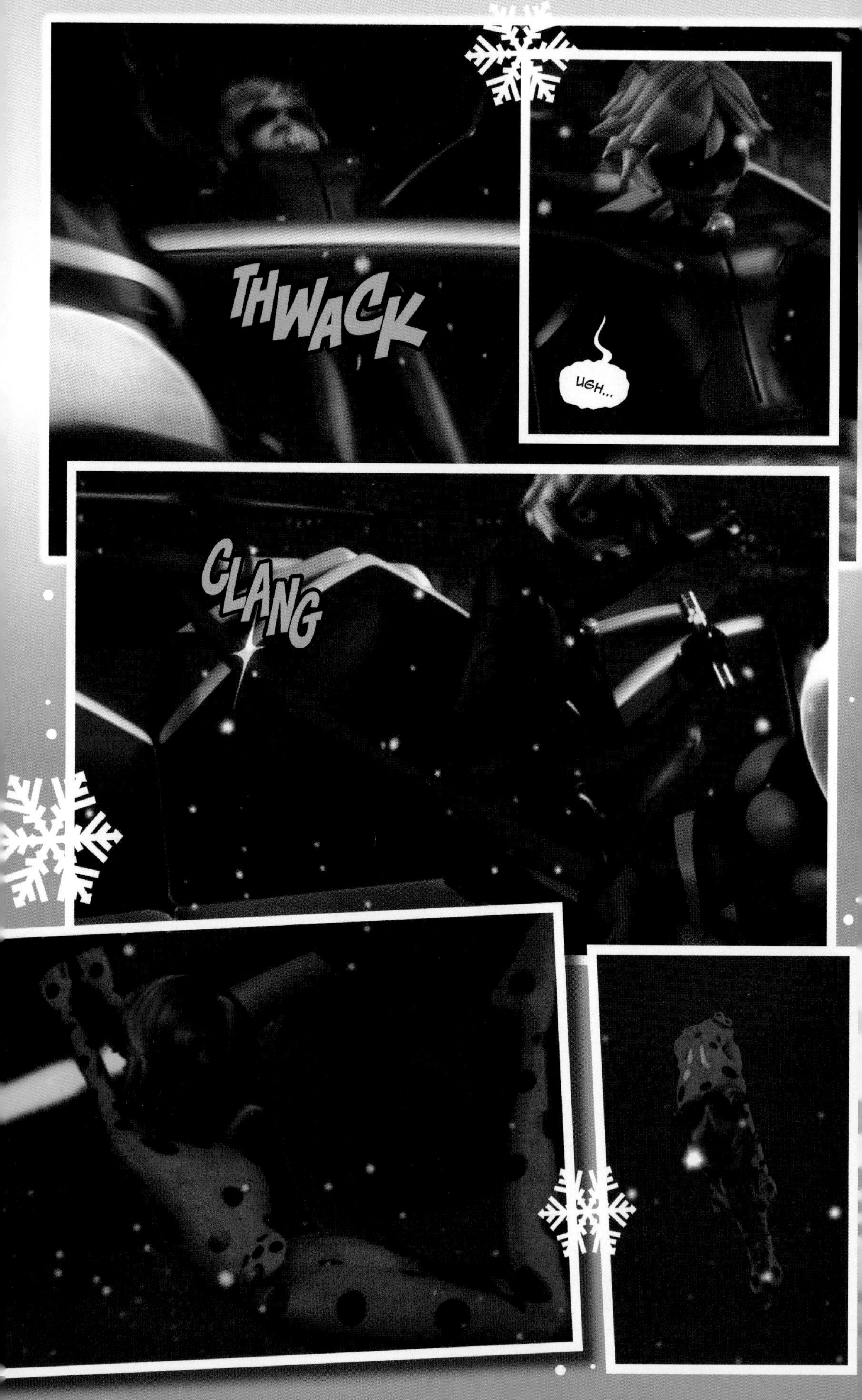
THWACK
UGH...
CLANG

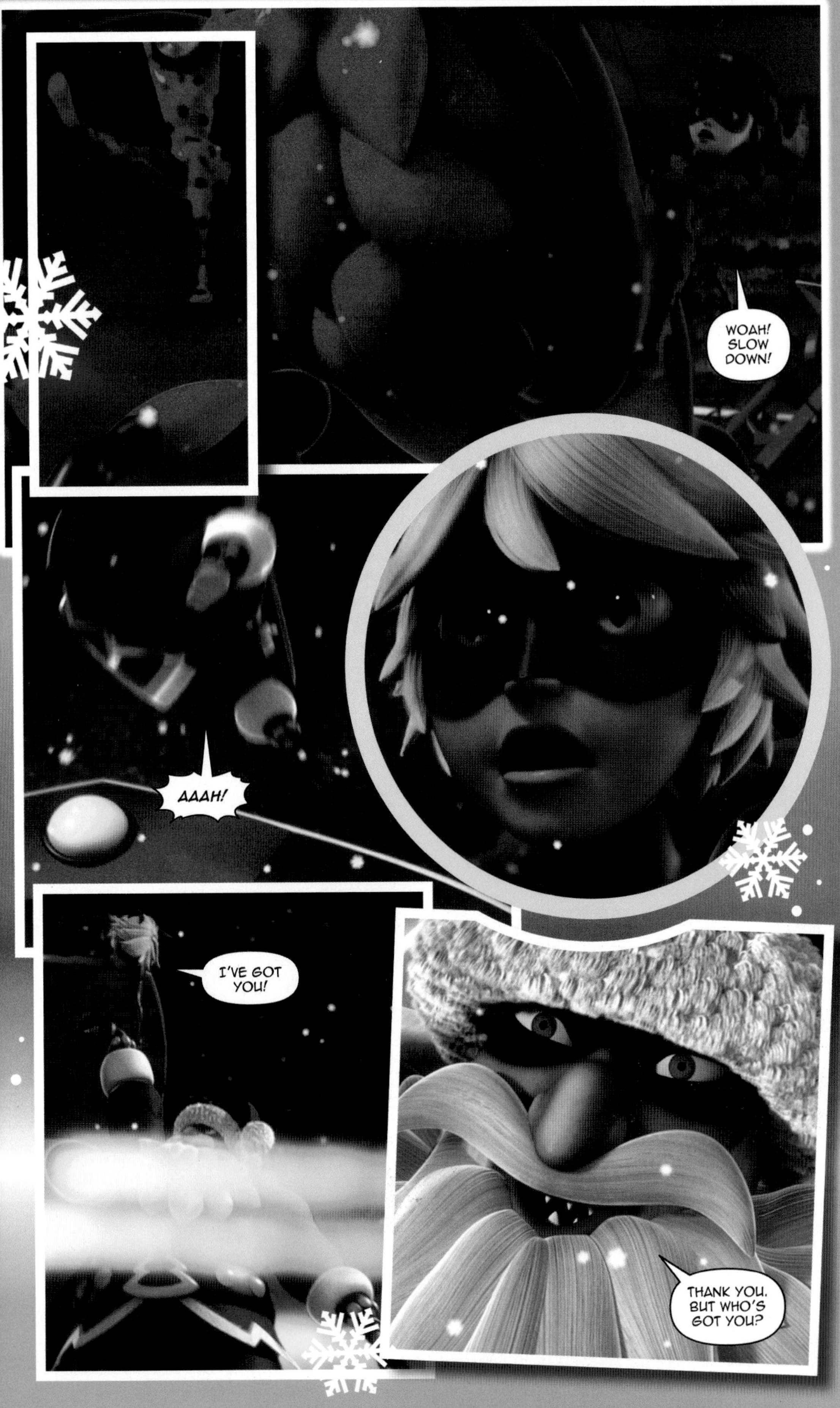
WOAH! SLOW DOWN!
AAAH!
I'VE GOT YOU!
THANK YOU. BUT WHO'S GOT YOU?

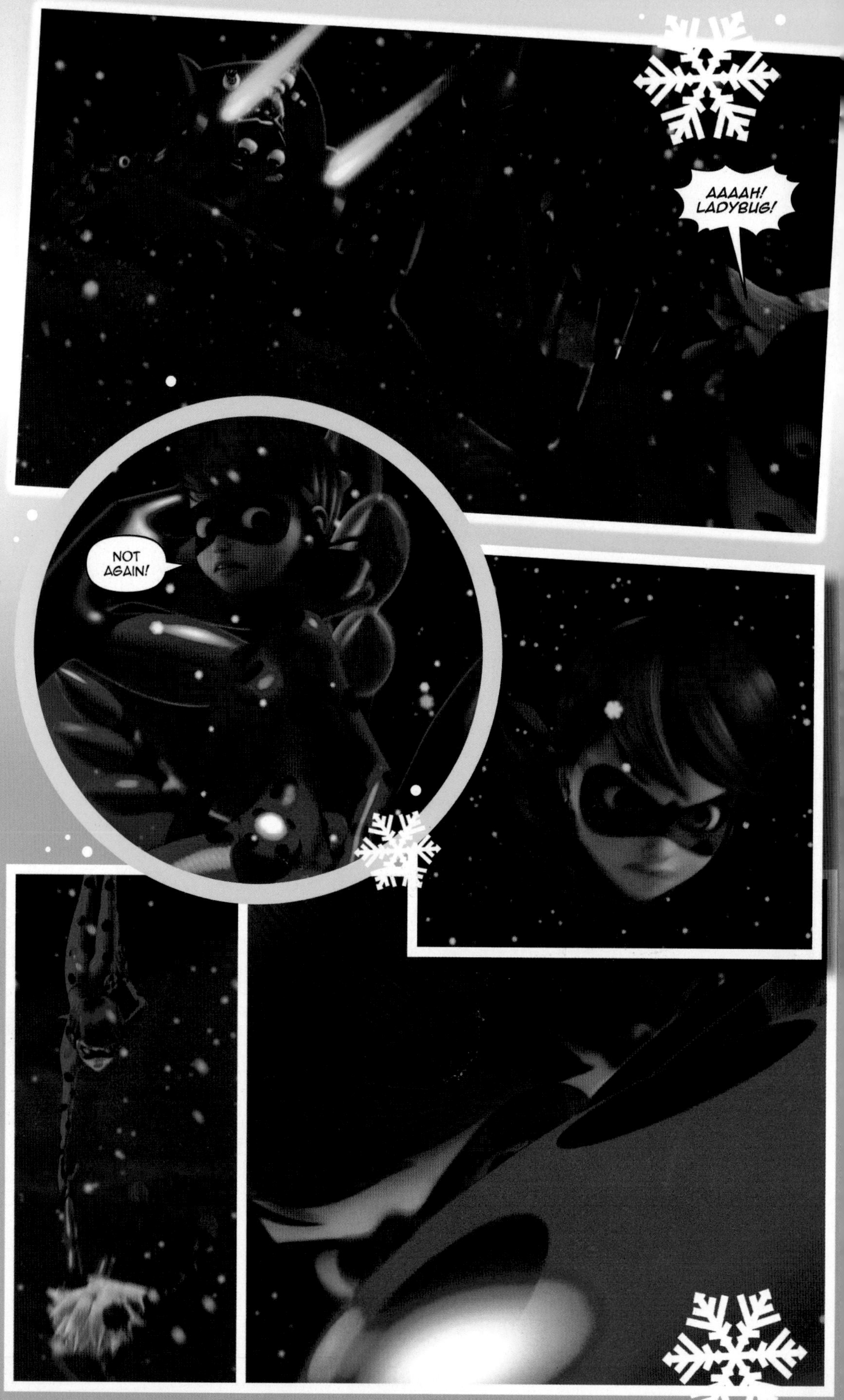
AAAAH! LADYBUG!
NOT AGAIN!

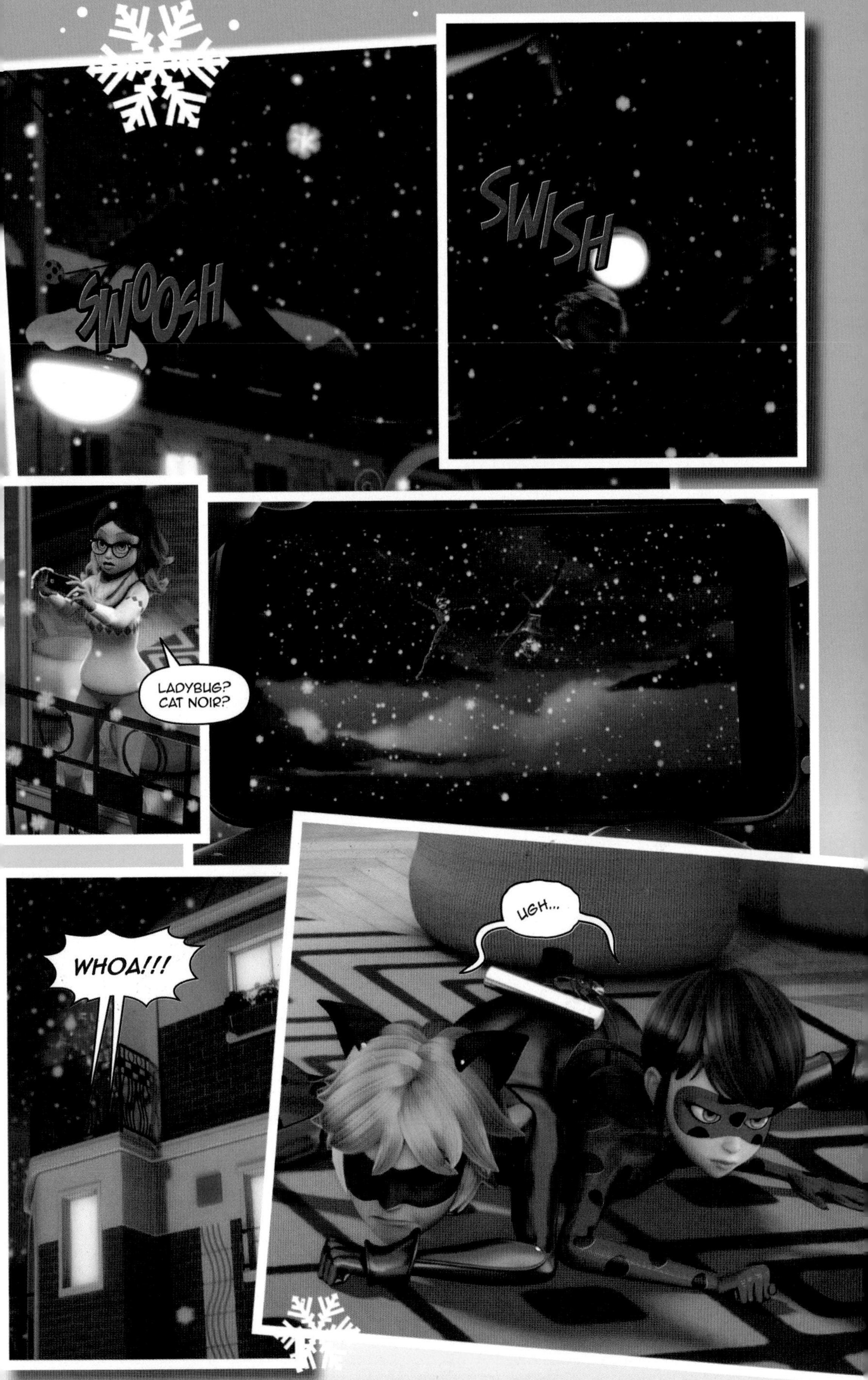
SWOOSH
SWISH
LADYBUG?
CAT NOIR?
WHOA!!!
UGH...

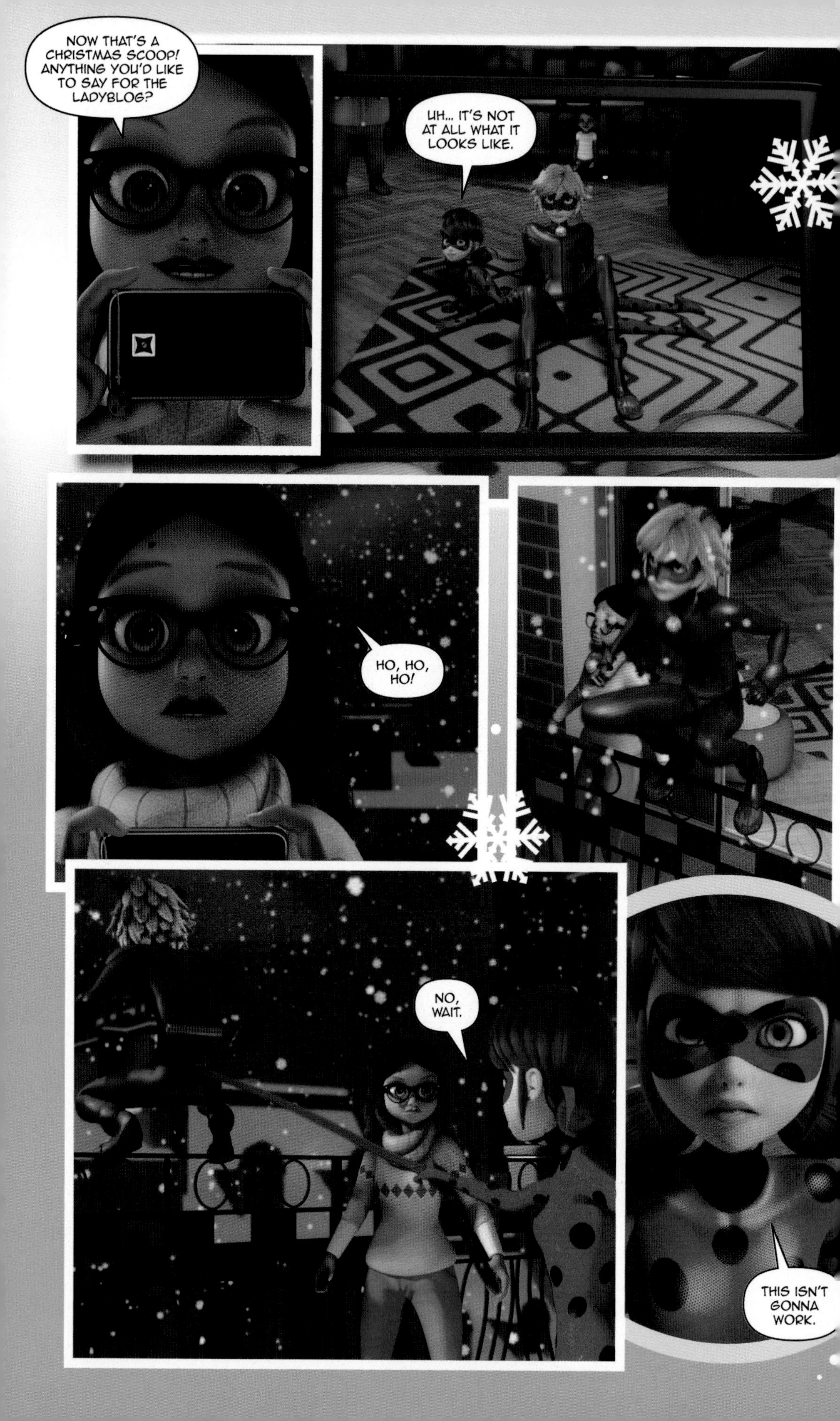
NOW THAT'S A CHRISTMAS SCOOP! ANYTHING YOU'D LIKE TO SAY FOR THE LADYBLOG?
UH... IT'S NOT AT ALL WHAT IT LOOKS LIKE.
HO, HO, HO!
NO, WAIT.
THIS ISN'T GONNA WORK.

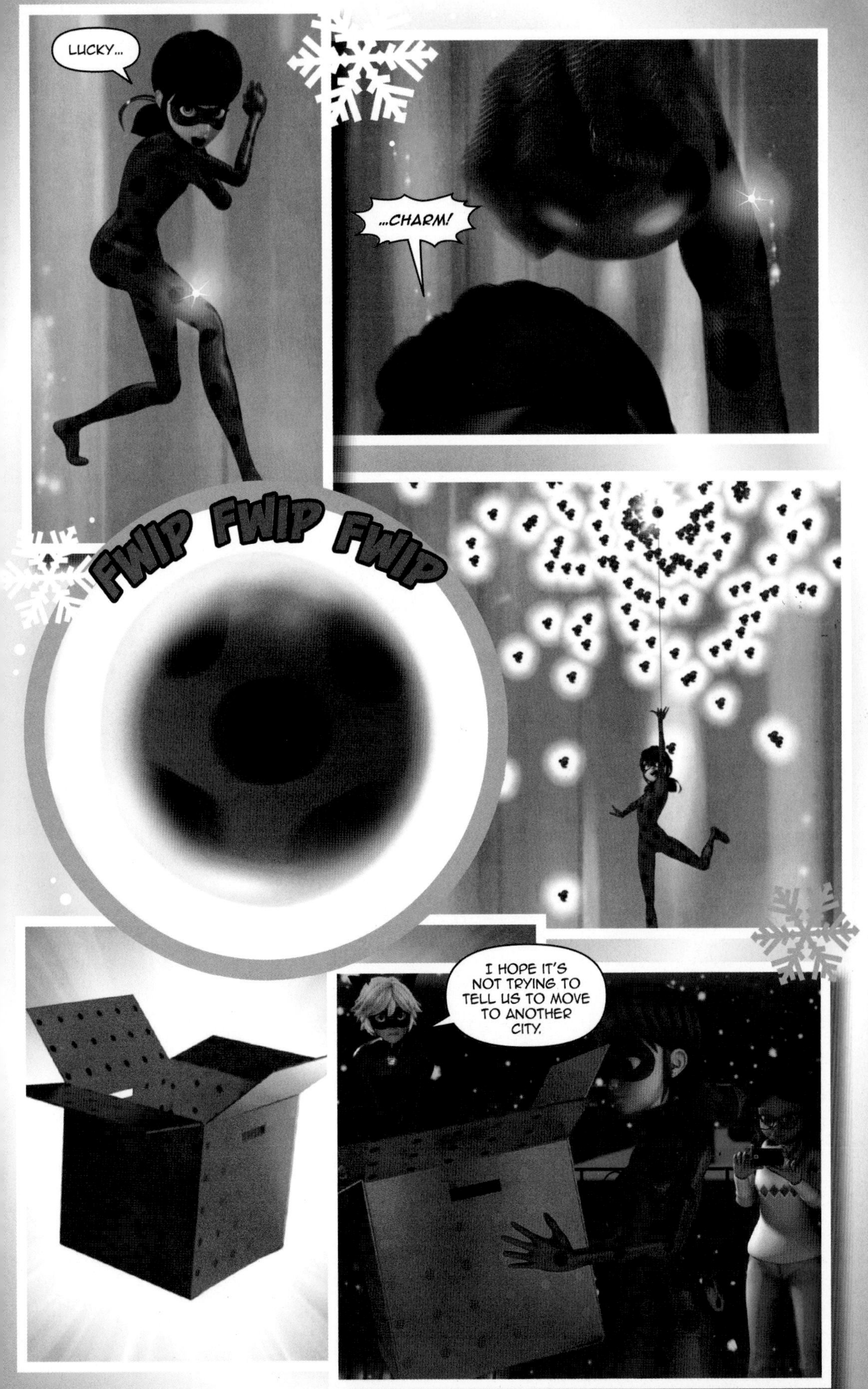
LUCKY...
...CHARM!
FWIP FWIP FWIP
I HOPE IT'S NOT TRYING TO TELL US TO MOVE TO ANOTHER CITY.

I NEED PACKING TAPE, SCISSORS AND OFFICE SUPPLIES. DO YOU GUYS HAVE THOSE THINGS HERE?
IN THERE!
DING
DING
RIGHT HERE.
DING
DING

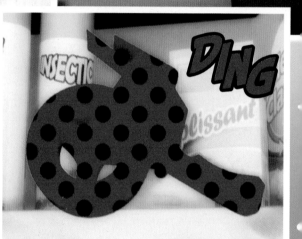

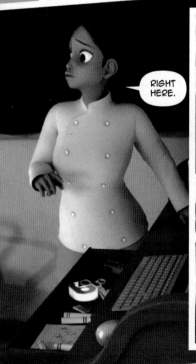

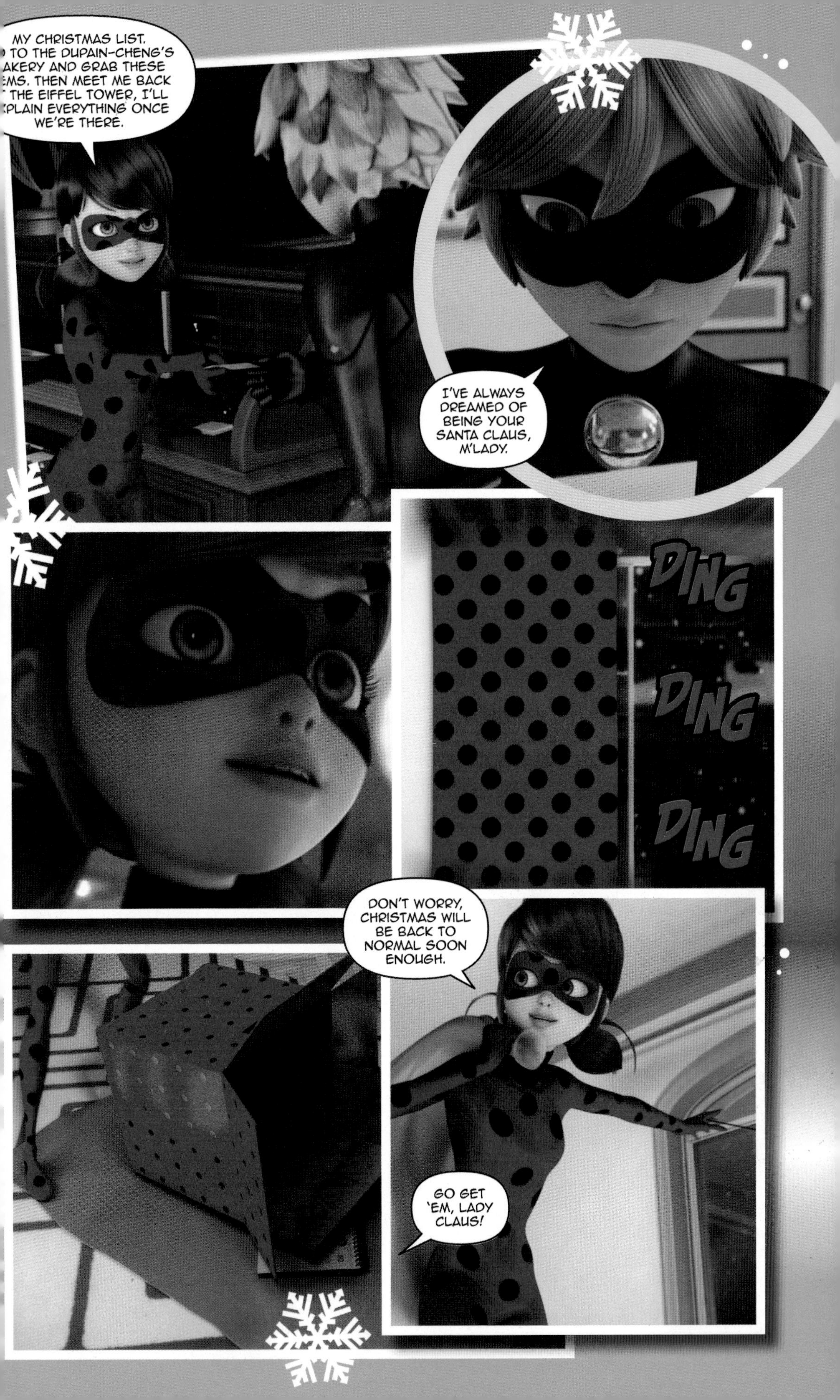
MY CHRISTMAS LIST. O TO THE DUPAIN-CHENG'S AKERY AND GRAB THESE EMS. THEN MEET ME BACK T THE EIFFEL TOWER, I'LL XPLAIN EVERYTHING ONCE WE'RE THERE.
I'VE ALWAYS DREAMED OF BEING YOUR SANTA CLAUS, M'LADY.
DING
DING
DING
DON'T WORRY, CHRISTMAS WILL BE BACK TO NORMAL SOON ENOUGH.
GO GET 'EM, LADY CLAUS!

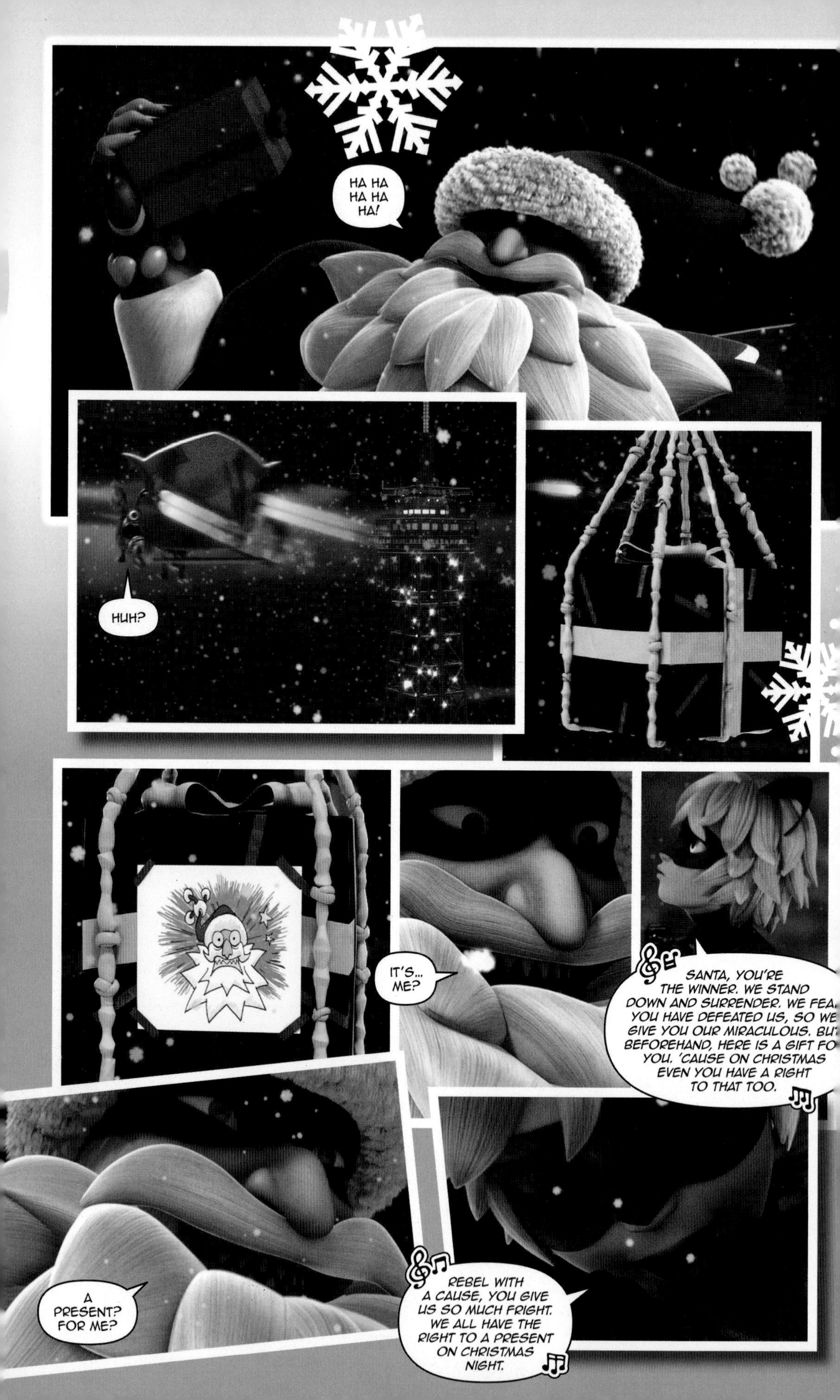

HA HA HA HA HA!
HUH?
IT'S... ME?
SANTA, YOU'RE THE WINNER. WE STAND DOWN AND SURRENDER. WE FEA YOU HAVE DEFEATED US, SO WE GIVE YOU OUR MIRACULOUS. BU BEFOREHAND, HERE IS A GIFT FO YOU. 'CAUSE ON CHRISTMAS EVEN YOU HAVE A RIGHT TO THAT TOO.
A PRESENT? FOR ME?
REBEL WITH A CAUSE, YOU GIVE US SO MUCH FRIGHT. WE ALL HAVE THE RIGHT TO A PRESENT ON CHRISTMAS NIGHT.

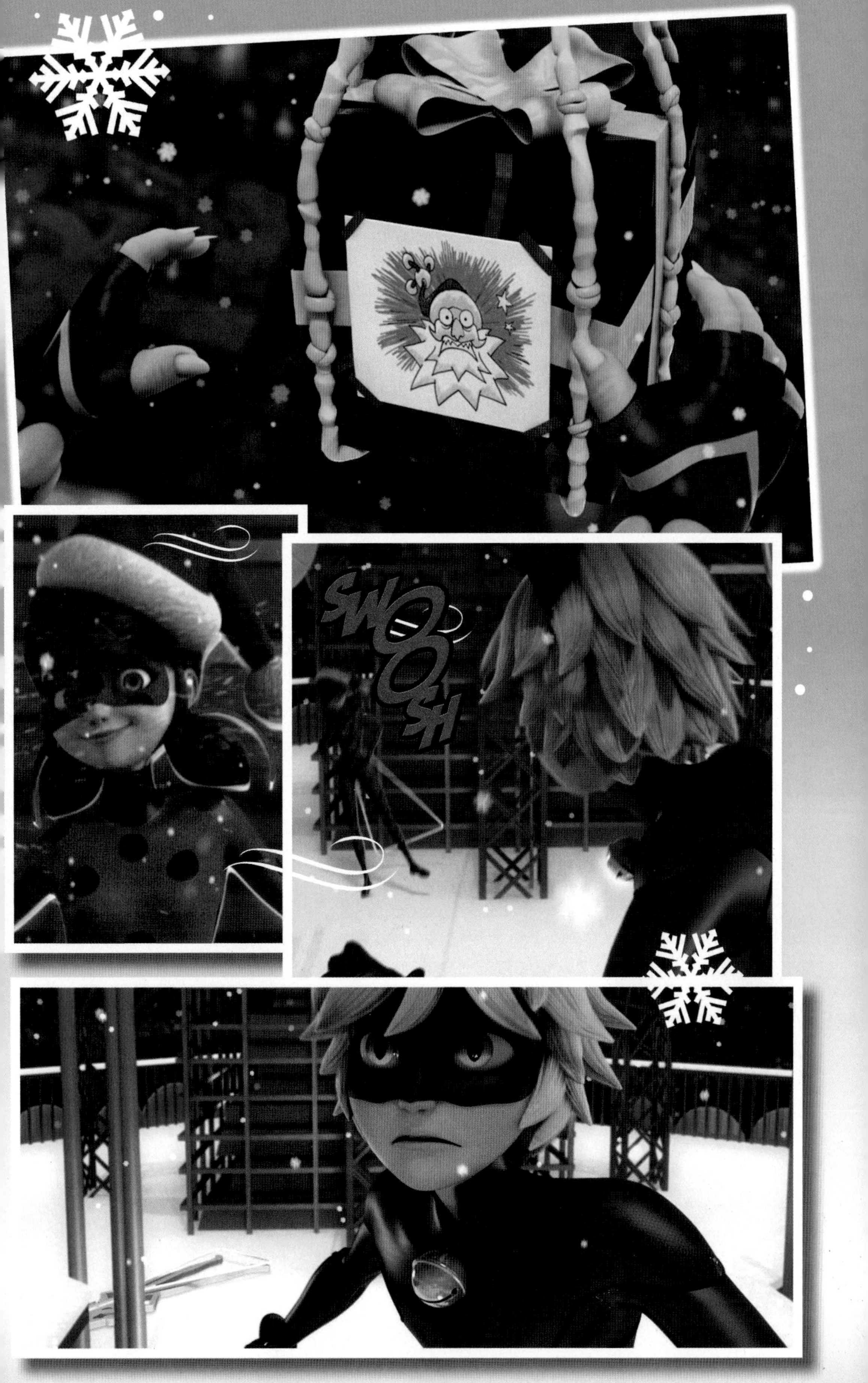
SWOOSH

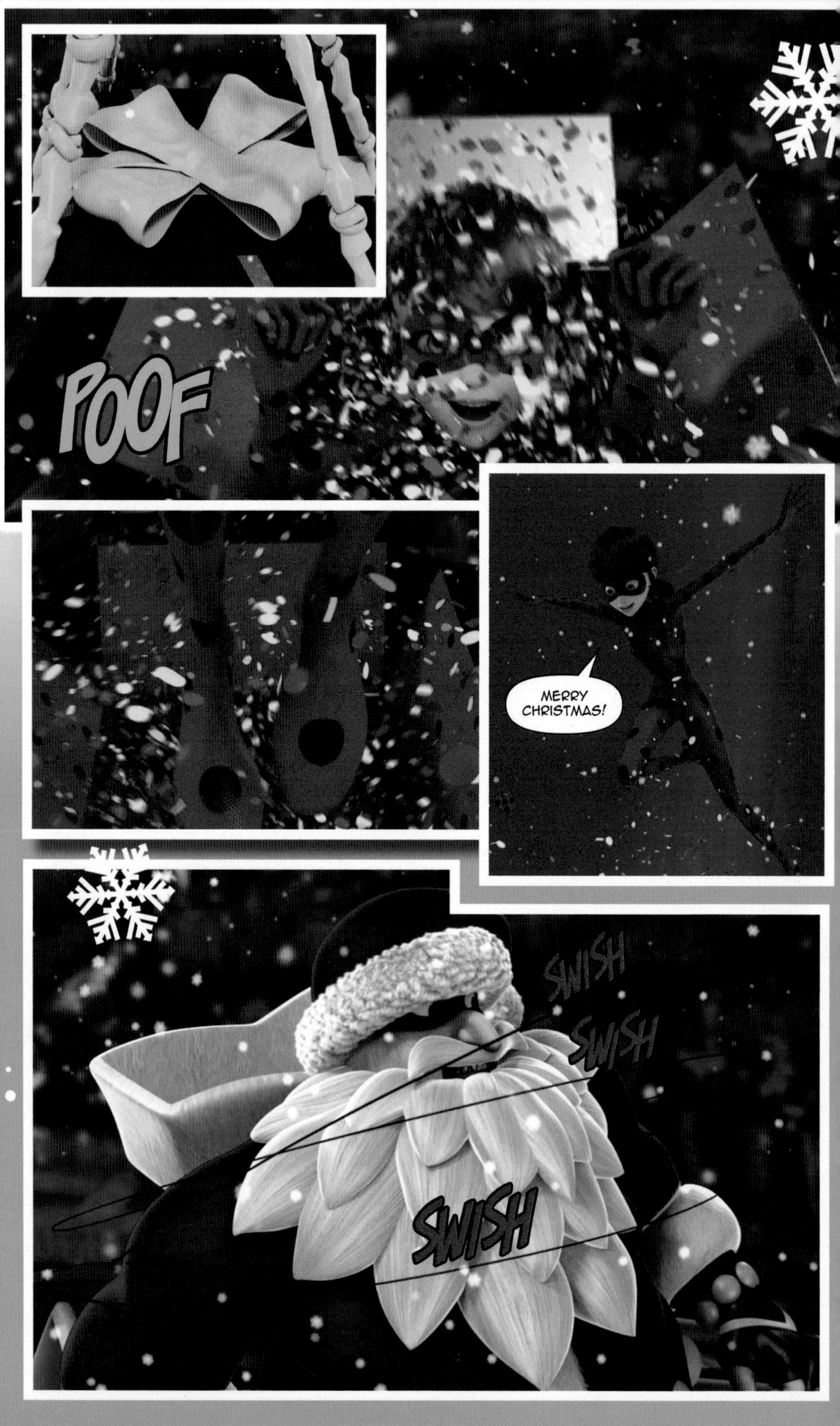
POOF
MERRY CHRISTMAS!
SWISH
SWISH
SWISH

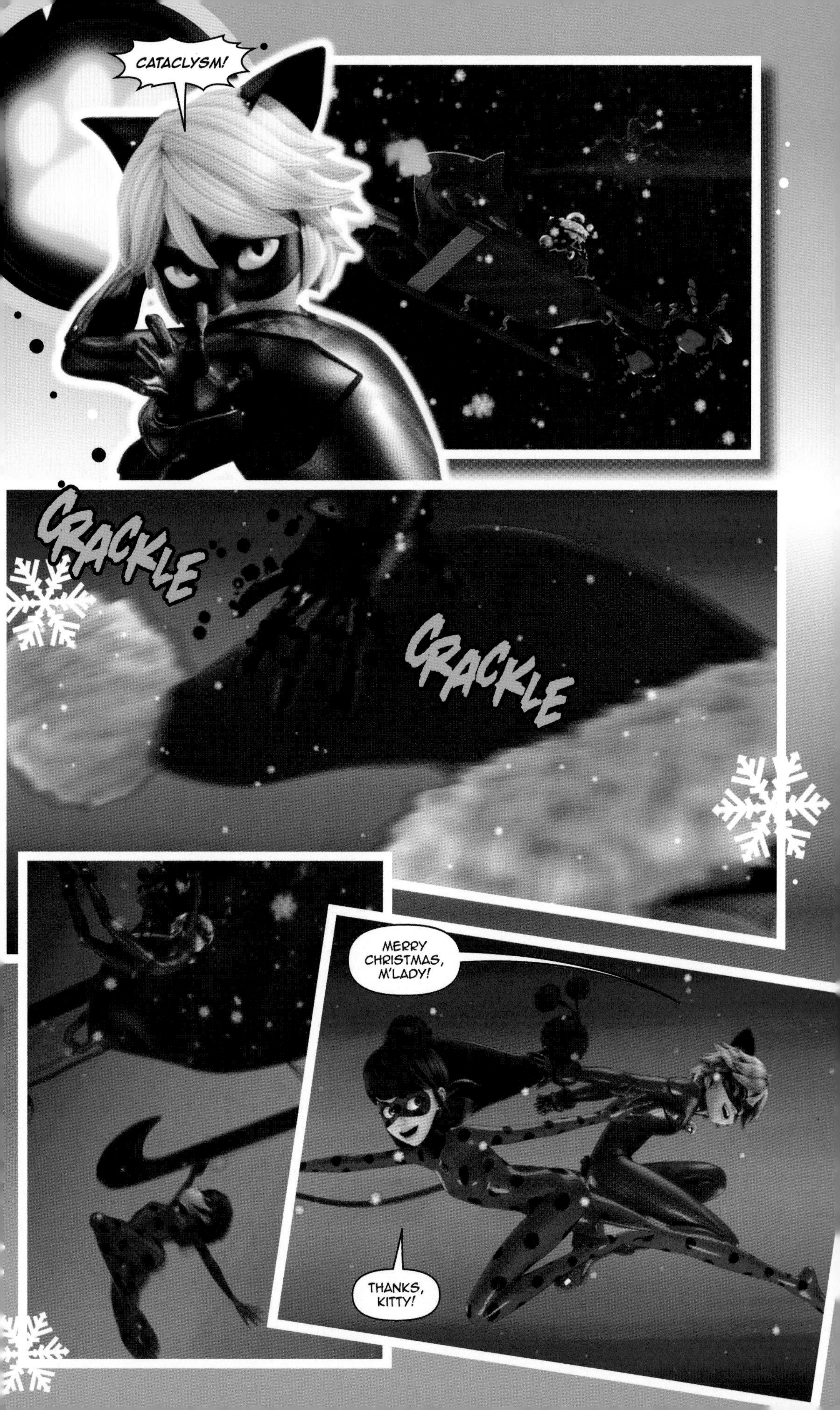
CATACLYSM!
CRACKLE
CRACKLE
MERRY CHRISTMAS, M'LADY!
THANKS, KITTY!

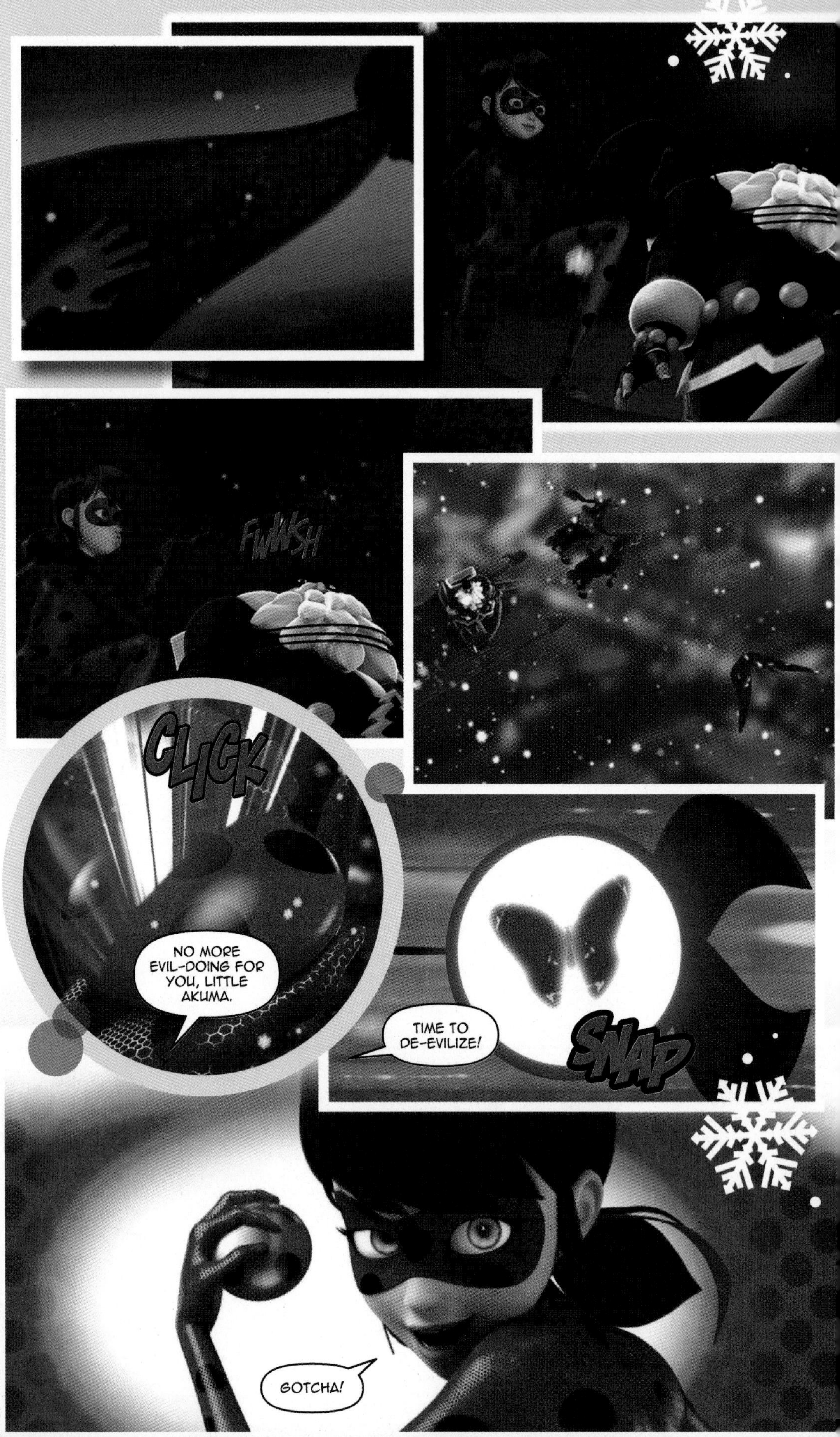
FWWSH
CLICK
NO MORE EVIL-DOING FOR YOU, LITTLE AKUMA.
TIME TO DE-EVILIZE!
SNAP
GOTCHA!

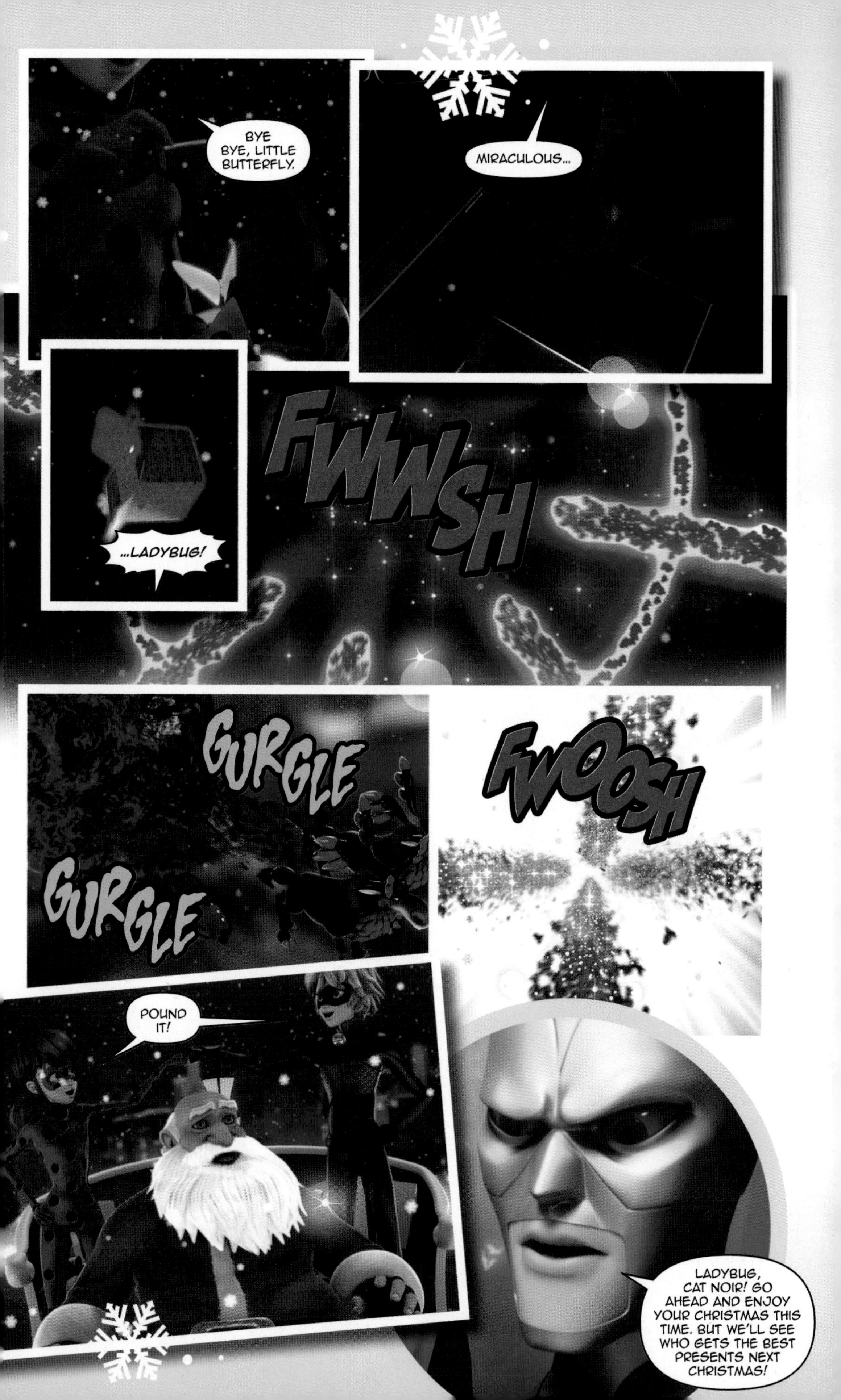

BYE BYE, LITTLE BUTTERFLY.
MIRACULOUS...
...LADYBUG!
FWWSH
GURGLE
GURGLE
FWOOSH
POUND IT!
LADYBUG, CAT NOIR! GO AHEAD AND ENJOY YOUR CHRISTMAS THIS TIME. BUT WE'LL SEE WHO GETS THE BEST PRESENTS NEXT CHRISTMAS!

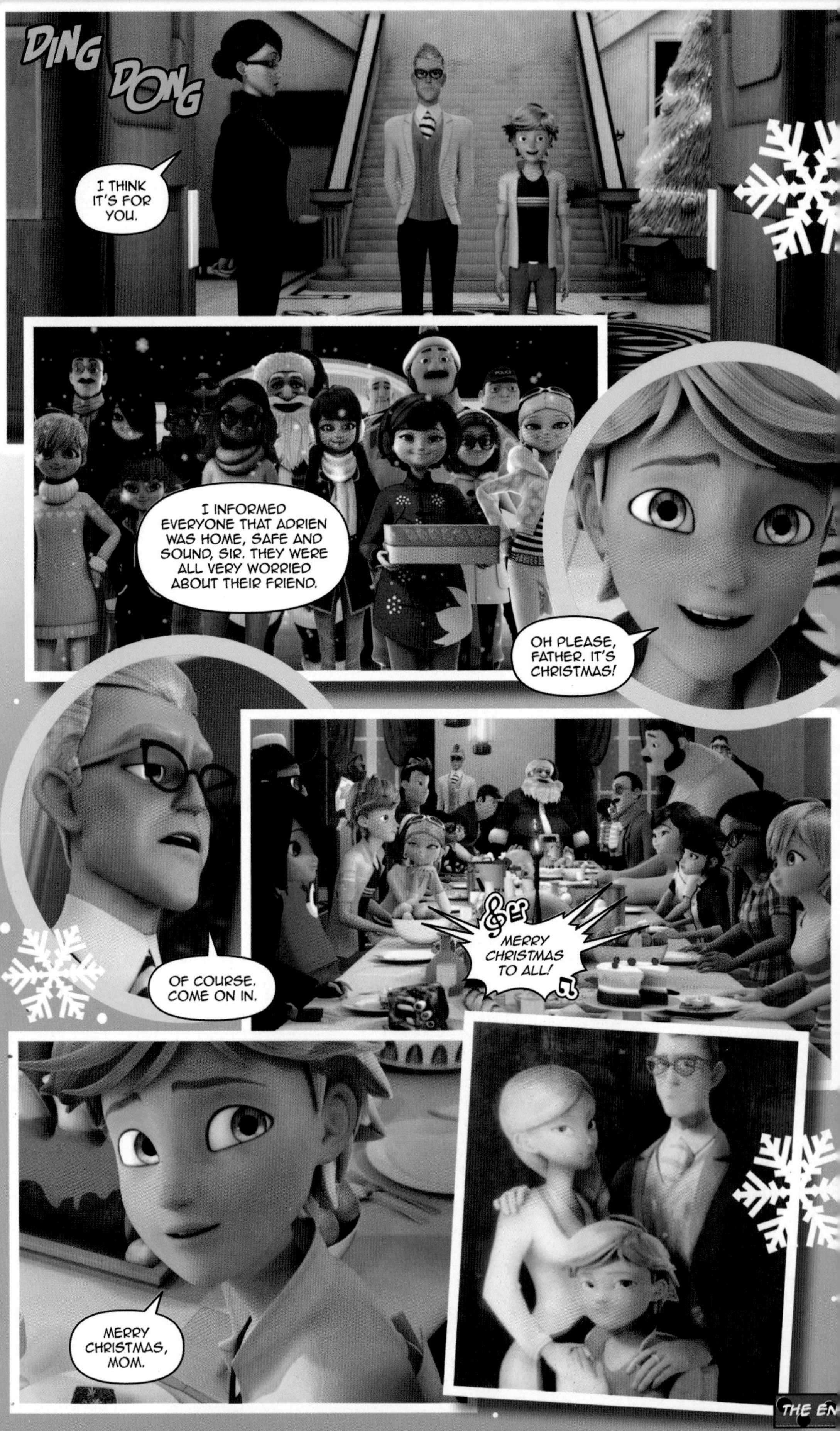
DING DONG
I THINK IT'S FOR YOU.
I INFORMED EVERYONE THAT ADRIEN WAS HOME, SAFE AND SOUND, SIR. THEY WERE ALL VERY WORRIED ABOUT THEIR FRIEND.
OH PLEASE, FATHER. IT'S CHRISTMAS!
OF COURSE. COME ON IN.
MERRY CHRISTMAS TO ALL!
MERRY CHRISTMAS, MOM.
THE EN

THE HIT ANIMATED SERIES COMES TO COMICS!

ZAG HEROEZ

Miraculous™

Tales of Ladybug & Cat Noir

Because of Ladybug, a Santa Claus gets akumatized by Hawk Moth. Now Santa Claws, he is determined to make this Christmas Eve the worst in Paris's history. Will Ladybug and Cat Noir manage to save Christmas?

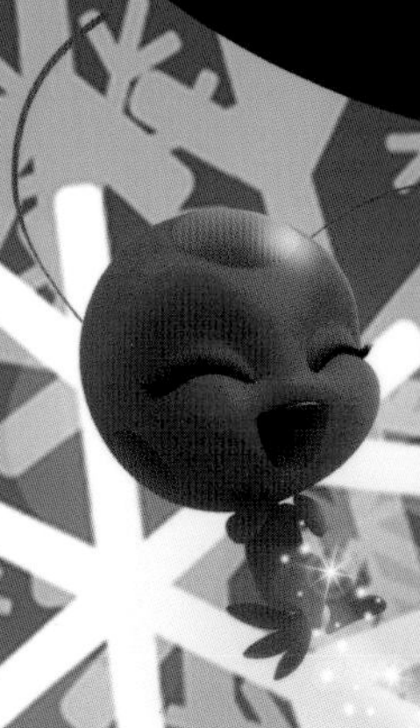

Miraculous - Santa Claws - Action Lab $6.99 USD
ISBN 978-1-63229-455-5 Higher in Canada
50699>
9 781632 294555

ALL-AGES $6.99 E

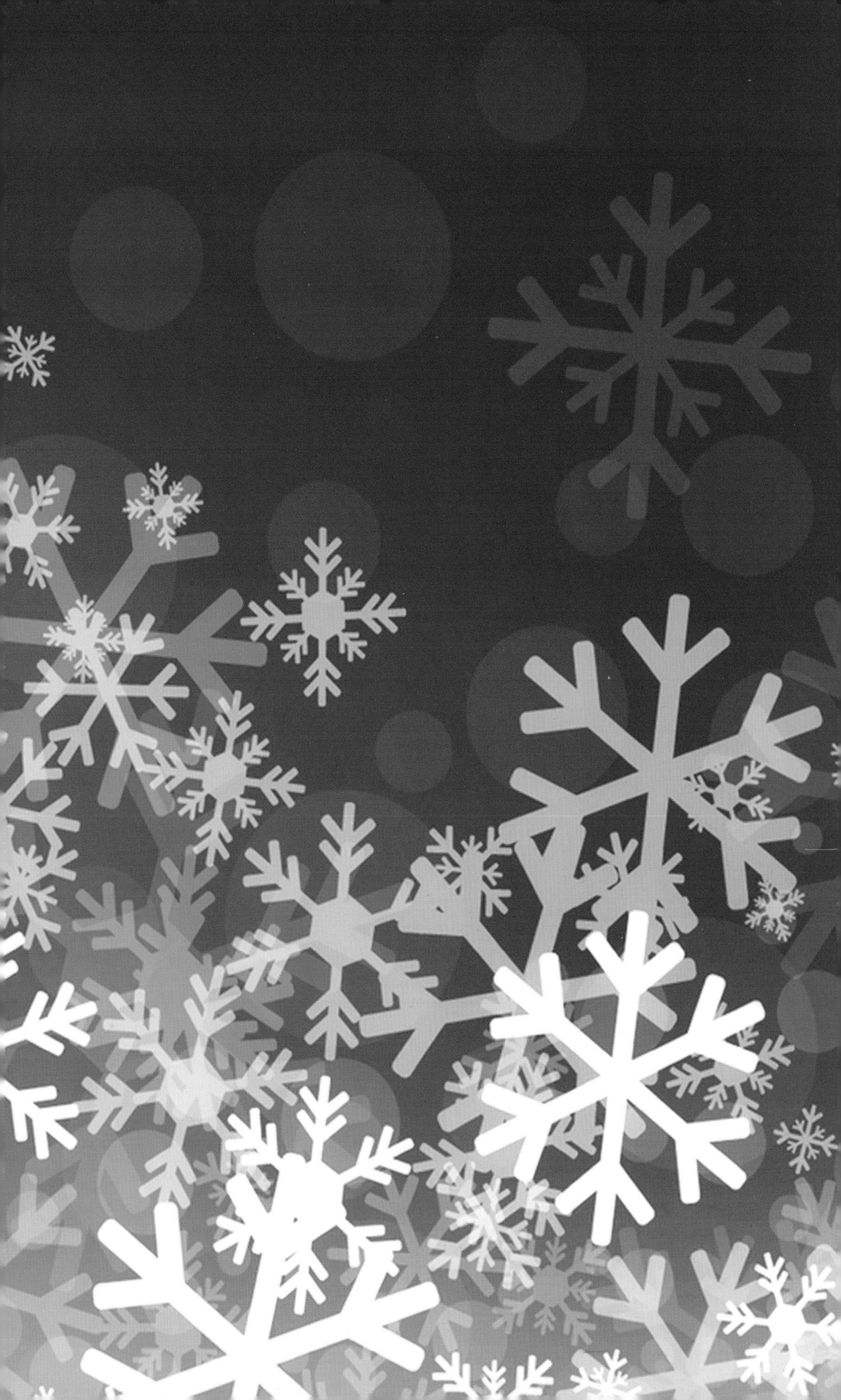

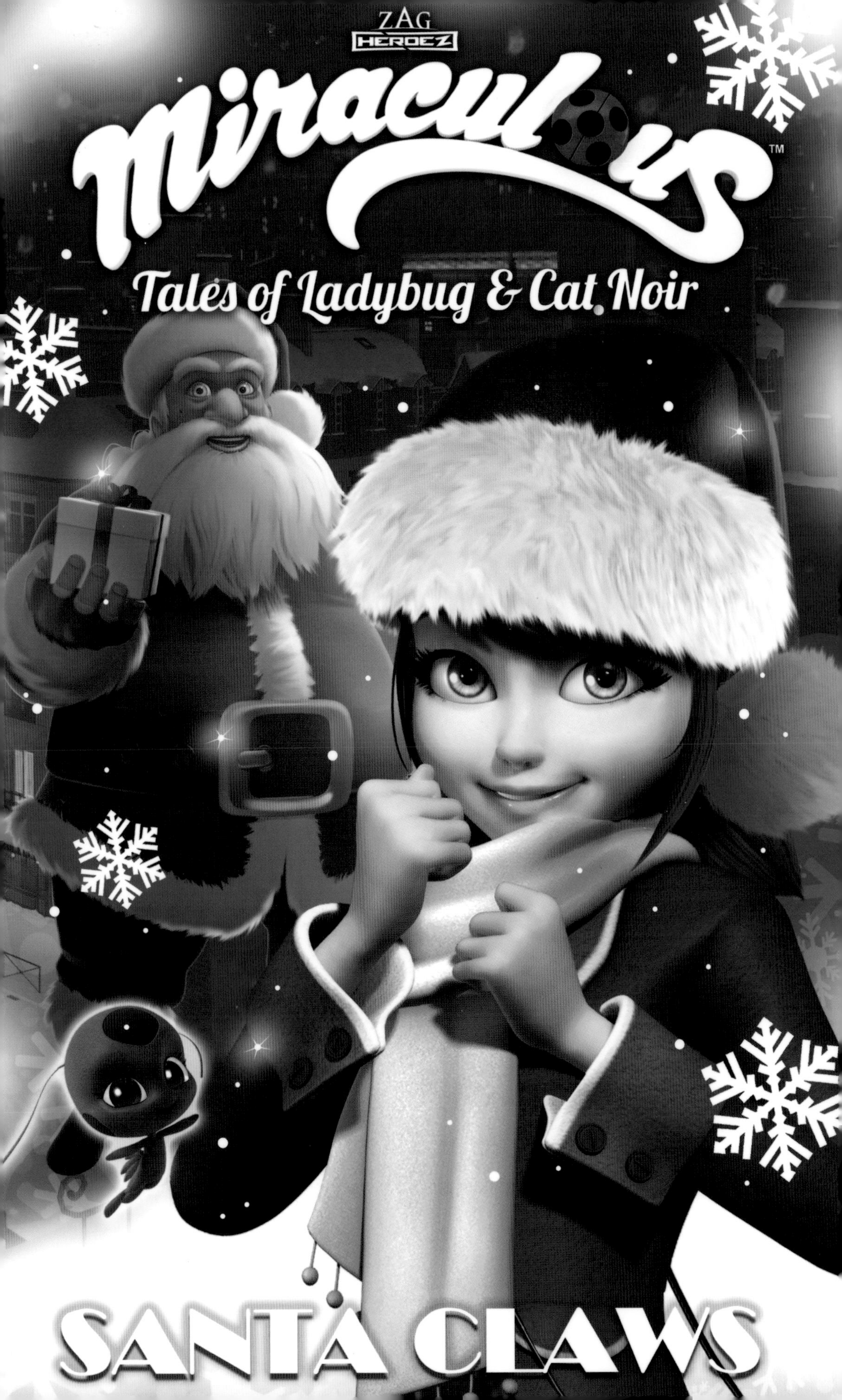
ZAG
HEROEZ
miraculous™
Tales of Ladybug & Cat Noir
SANTA CLAWS

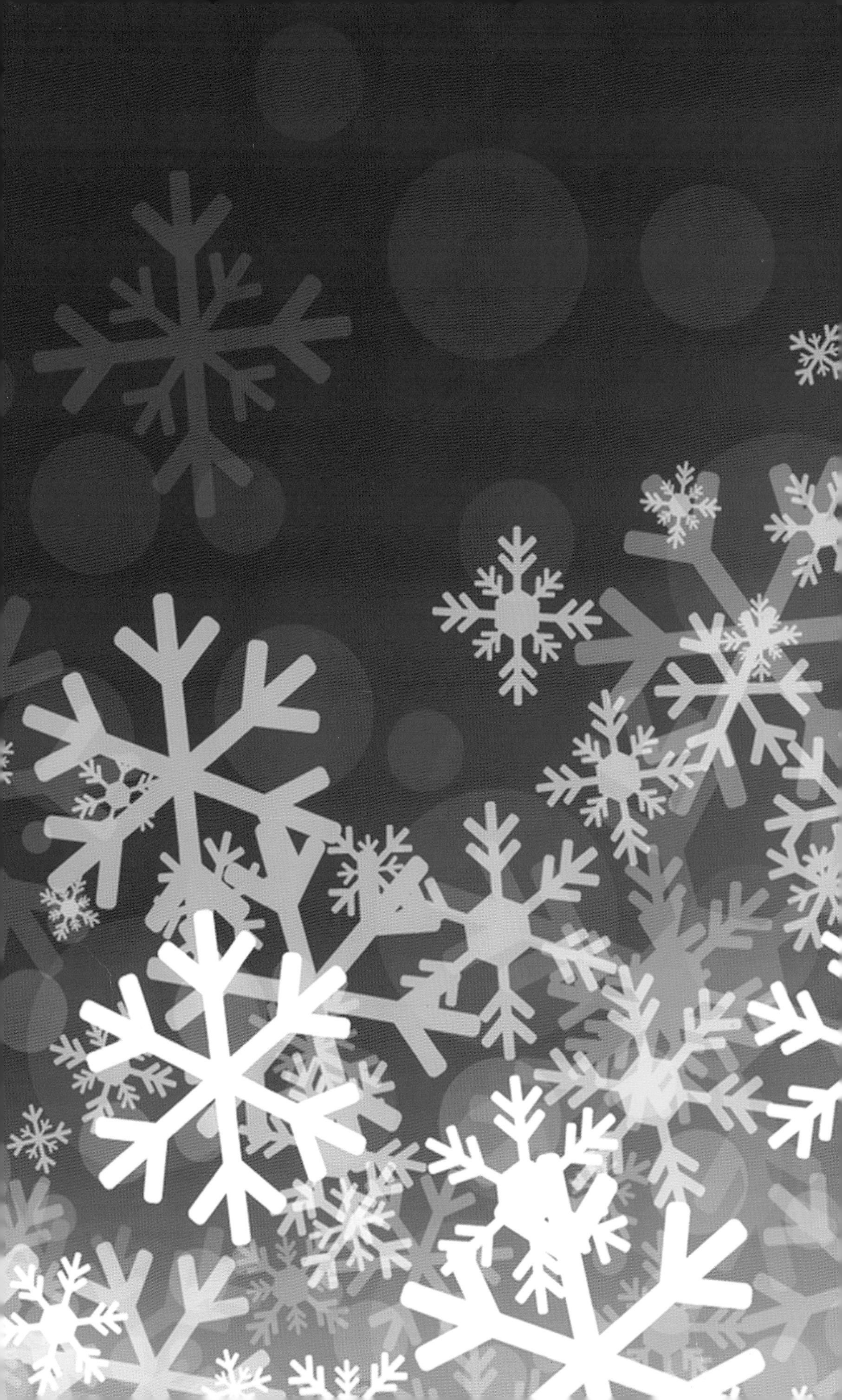